Richard Stark is one of the pseudonyms of prolific writer Donald E. Westlake. Many of his books have been made into movies, including *The Hunter* and *Payback*. He penned the Hollywood scripts for *The Stepfather* and *The Grifters*, and has won three Edgar awards and a Mystery Writers of America Grand Master. Donald E. Westlake lives with his wife, Abby Adams, in rural New York State.

NOBODY RUNS FOREVER

When a larger bank takes over a smaller bank it's called a merger. When all the cash and assets of the smaller bank are moved in the dead of night to be taken to the vaults of the larger bank, Parker calls it an opportunity. With two professionals and an amateur inside source on his side, the only thing that stands between Parker and the money is four armoured trucks. He has everything he needs but eyes in the back of his head — and he's going to need them too.

RICHARD STARK

NOBODY RUNS FOREVER

Complete and Unabridged

ULVERSCROFT
Leicester

First published in Great Britain in 2005 by
Robert Hale Limited
London

First Large Print Edition
published 2006
by arrangement with
Robert Hale Limited
London

The moral right of the author has been asserted

This book is a work of fiction. Names, characters, places and incidents are the product of the author's imagination or are used fictitiously.
Any resemblance to actual events, locales, or persons, living or dead, is coincidental.

British Library CIP Data

Stark, Richard, *1933 –*
    Nobody runs forever.—Large print ed.—
Ulverscroft large print series: crime
    1. Parker (Fictitious character)—Fiction
    2. Bank robberies—Fiction
    3. Detective and mystery stories 4. Large type books
I. Title
813.5′4 [F]

    ISBN 1–84617–558–5

Published by
F. A. Thorpe (Publishing)
Anstey, Leicestershire

Set by Words & Graphics Ltd.
Anstey, Leicestershire
Printed and bound in Great Britain by
T. J. International Ltd., Padstow, Cornwall

This book is printed on acid-free paper

ONE

1

When he saw that the one called Harbin was wearing a wire, Parker said, 'Deal me out a hand,' and got to his feet. They'd all come to this late-night meeting in suits and ties, traveling businessmen taking a break with a little seven-card stud. Harbin, a nervous man unused to the dress shirt, kept twitching and moving around, bending forward to squint at his cards, and finally Parker, a quarter around the table to Harbin's left, saw in the gap between shirt buttons that flash of clear tape holding the wire down.

As he walked around the table, Parker stripped off his own tie — dark blue with thin gold stripes — slid it into a double thickness, and arched it over Harbin's head. He drew the two ends through the loop and yanked back hard with his right hand as his body pressed both Harbin and the chair he was in against the table, and his left hand reached over to rip open Harbin's shirt. The other five at the table, about to speak or move or react to what Parker was doing, stopped when they saw the wire taped to Harbin's pale chest, the edge of the black metal box taped to his side.

Parker bore down, holding Harbin against the table, pulling back now with both hands on the tie, twisting the tie. Harbin's hands, imprisoned in his lap, beat a drumroll on the bottom of the table. The other players held the table in place, palms down, and looked at McWhitney, red-bearded and red-faced, who'd brought Harbin here. McWhitney, expression solemn, looked around at each face and shook his head; he hadn't known.

'My deal, I think,' Dalesia said, as calm as before, and shuffled the cards a while, as the others watched Harbin and Parker. Dalesia dealt out hands in front of himself, all the cards facedown, and said, 'Bet the king.'

'Fold,' said Mott.

It was Stratton who'd taken this hotel room in Cincinnati. He pointed at McWhitney, pointed at Harbin, made a thumb gesture like an umpire calling the runner out. McWhitney nodded and quietly got to his feet, being sure the chair wouldn't scrape on the floor.

Mott and Fletcher were seated flanking Harbin; now they held him upright while Parker peeled his necktie out of the new, deep crease in Harbin's neck.

'These cards are dead,' Mott said, and Fletcher peeled the tape off Harbin's chest, freeing the antenna wire and the transmitter box.

McWhitney, standing there, made a broad shrugging gesture to the table, a combination of apology and innocence, then came around to pick Harbin up in a fireman's carry, bent forward with Harbin's forearms looped around his own throat.

'Bet two,' Parker said, coming back to his place at the table.

Fletcher held the transmitter and antenna while Mott crossed to the sofa at the side of the room and came back with a cushion, which he put where Harbin had been seated. Fletcher put the transmitter on the cushion, and they all sat, making comments about the game they weren't playing, except Stratton, who went into the other room, where his gear was.

McWhitney carried Harbin to the hall door, looked out, and left, carrying the body. At twenty after one on a weekday morning, there wasn't likely to be much traffic out there.

They continued not to play, to discuss how cold the cards were, and to suggest they might all make an early night of it. They hadn't been together in the room long before Parker had made his discovery, and so hadn't yet started to talk about anything that the wire shouldn't know. They were mostly new to one another, and would have had to get

5

acquainted a while before they started to talk for real.

Stratton was back from the other room in five minutes, with one suitcase. He took his former chair and said, 'Deal me out.'

The others all made comments about breaking up early, the cards not interesting, try again some other time. Fletcher, who, it turned out, could sound something like Harbin, with that same rasp in his voice, said, 'You guys go ahead, I'll clean up in here.'

'Thanks, Harbin,' Stratton said, and as they left, they all said, 'See you, Harbin,' to the transmitter on the cushion.

2

Parker and Dalesia and Fletcher and Mott and Stratton rode the elevator down together. Mott said, 'Which of us is in their sights, do you think?'

'I hope not me,' Stratton said. 'I took that room. Not as me, but still . . . '

Parker said, 'Most likely McWhitney, he brought him.'

'Or maybe,' Fletcher said, 'just any target of opportunity. Decorate him like a Christmas tree, send him out to get them somebody else, because they've already got him.'

'That sounds right,' Stratton said. 'They love to turn people. Tag, you're it, now you're on my side, go turn some of your friends.'

'They're like vampires,' Fletcher said, 'making more vampires.'

The lobby door opened and they went out to a big space empty of people except for one green-blazered girl clerk behind the check-in desk. Fletcher and Mott had come together, and went off together. The other three had all arrived alone. 'See you,' Stratton said and left.

Parker was also going to leave, but Nick Dalesia said, 'You got a minute?'

7

Dalesia, a thin man with tense shoulders, was the one who'd invited Parker here, and the only one present he'd known before, and that not very well. 'Yes,' Parker said.

'Let's find a bar.'

*   *   *

At a booth in an underpopulated bar, the few other customers either male — female couples or male singletons, Dalesia said, 'This means I'm still out of work.'

'Yes,' Parker said.

'And you, too.'

Parker shrugged.

Dalesia said, 'I came here because the only other thing I had for a possible is maybe a little iffy and farther down the line. But now I'm thinking maybe I'll look into it, and maybe you'd like to check it out, too. It's good to have somebody with you where there's a little history.'

'Not much history,' Parker said.

Nick Dalesia was a driver brought into a job Parker was on some years ago, brought in there by a guy named Tom Hurley, who Parker had known better. But Hurley got himself shot in the arm that time, and hadn't ever gotten over it completely, and had gone away to life in retirement somewhere offshore, maybe the Caribbean. Dalesia had been competent that one time, but Parker hadn't met up with him again until Dalesia had made the phone call that had brought them both here.

'A little history is enough,' Dalesia said, 'if you feel you can trust the guy. This gold thing is dead, I think.' Meaning Stratton's target, which they hadn't gotten around to talking about: a shipment of dental gold.

'It's dead as far as I'm concerned,' Parker said. 'What's this other thing?'

'It's a bank,' Dalesia said, 'in western Massachusetts.'

Parker shook his head. 'A small-town bank? There's not much there.'

'No, what this is,' Dalesia told him, 'it's a transfer of assets. These two local banks merged, or one of them bought the other one, so they're shutting one of the main offices down, so they're emptying a vault.'

'Heavy security,' Parker said.

'You're right.'

Parker frowned toward the bar. 'The reason it's iffy,' he said, 'is it comes with somebody inside.'

'Right again.'

'You know,' Parker said, 'the amateur on the inside is what usually makes a good thing go bad.'

9

'What they're doing,' Dalesia said, 'they're doing an all-night move, four armored vans, state police, private security. Moving everything, the bank's records, the commercial paper, the cash. What Mrs Inside gives us is not only what night do they do it, but which van has the cash.'

'Mrs Inside?'

'The wife of the bank that's being merged,' Dalesia said. 'Don't ask me what her problem is. The point is, nobody can take down four armored cars in a convoy, and what are the odds of getting the right one? But if you *know* the right one, chances are, you can cherry-pick it.'

'And if that happens,' Parker said, 'not only do they know there was somebody on the inside, pretty soon they know who.'

'But she won't lead them to us,' Dalesia said, 'because she doesn't know us. Who she knows is a guy used to work security for the bank, like head of all the guards or something — he skimmed a little too often, did time. That bent him over to our side, he's been in a few things, I got to know him, Jake Beckham. Mean anything?'

'Never heard of him.'

'Good, so you're even further away. The wife went to Beckham, offered him the job for a piece, he came to me, and I made the exact same face you're making right now. But Stratton's gold mine isn't gonna happen, so I'm thinking I'll call Beckham, see if it's all still the same. Will you want to hear what he says?'

'I can listen,' Parker said.

3

Parker drove the MassPike east out of New York State and pulled off at the service area just west of Huntington, getting there a little before three in the afternoon. It was mid-September, the air crisp, the sunlight sharp, like a clean blade. He put his Lexus in among the tourists' cars and got out to stretch. He was a few minutes early, but after driving up from New Jersey, he was ready to stand.

Over there to his right, the MassPike roared, heavy traffic in both directions. That was the easternmost leg of Interstate 90, beginning on the Atlantic coast at Boston and ending three thousand miles to the west in Seattle. This part of the road was always busy, the big rigs and the tourists and the commuters streaming along together, everybody at eighty, holding inside their own bubble of space in the flow or there'd be hell to pay.

He was there five minutes when a green Audi eased down the lane between the rows of parked cars and came to a stop. Parker nodded at Dalesia at the wheel and walked around the car to get in on the passenger side. Dalesia put the Audi in gear and said, 'Well, even if it turns out to be nothing, we've got good weather for it.'

There was nothing to say to that, so Parker watched as Dalesia put them back up on the Pike, eastbound, then said, 'Where we headed?'

'Exit's about fifteen miles farther on, near Westfield. Then we turn north. Was that your car back there, or just something you picked up?'

'Mine.'

'Then we'll come back for it.'

★ ★ ★

Once they got off the MassPike, Dalesia took them on increasingly narrow winding roads as they headed northwest. 'All the real roads around here,' he explained as they stopped at and then crossed another larger road, 'want to take you east, over to the towns along the Connecticut River. What we want is north, up near Vermont.'

They rode a few minutes in silence, and then Dalesia said, 'I heard a little more about what happened after we left.'

Parker said, 'Stratton and his dental gold?'

'Yeah.'

13

'Stratton was the one brought you in, wasn't he?'

'Oh, yeah, it was his party. I called him a few days later.'

'On this thing we're going to?' Parker wouldn't like that.

Dalesia shook his head. 'No,' he said, leaning on it. 'If you make a meet, and one guy shows up wired, anybody could be the hot one, starting with the host.'

'And including you or me.'

'Well, not so much,' Dalesia said. 'You didn't know anybody there but me, and I didn't know anybody but you and Stratton. So what I wanted to know was, were they looking at me now, just in case Stratton had been their first target. According to him, the very next day after we decided not to play poker after all, some state cops scooped up McWhitney.'

'He's the one brought Harbin.'

'That's right. Apparently, these cops were a little pissed. Their boy Harbin wasn't anywhere to be found, and McWhitney must have been their target, since he's who they went after right away. But they didn't have anything. If he'd wanted to negotiate, McWhitney had a name or two on us, mostly wrong, but mostly all he had to do was tell them he didn't know anything about

14

anything. They had no probable cause, no specific crime, not even a discussion. Just a wire left behind in an empty room. So he's out.'

'With a leash on him,' Parker said.

'Oh, sure.' Dalesia shrugged and said, 'I figure Stratton's got a leash, too, these days, since he's the one called McWhitney for the meet.'

'If they think there's something to be found,' Parker said, 'they'll look behind Stratton. They'll want to know who else was in that room.'

'Here's the funny thing,' Dalesia said. 'They can't get to you except through me, because Stratton didn't know you from a bag of Bugler, and they can't get to me except through Stratton, because the rest of them were new to me. But that doesn't help them either, because I don't know Stratton's first name, and he doesn't know my last.' Grinning, he said, 'I mean, he *really* doesn't know it. You remember, in the room, he introduced me as Nick.'

'I remember.'

Dalesia negotiated a steep climbing curve, moving up into the Hoosac hills, trending northwest toward the Berkshires. Then he said, 'You'd be surprised how many people there are named Nick.'

4

The town was called Rutherford, built into a lower south-facing fold of the Berkshires. Vermont was another ten or fifteen miles farther north, New York State a little farther to the west. The town apparently had some seasonal tourist business because of ski slopes nearby, judging from the few specialty shops along the main street, but this wasn't the season yet, and the place had a siesta look to it.

Driving slowly along toward the town's only traffic light, the time now about four-thirty in the afternoon, Dalesia said, 'We're looking for a doctor, on the right, a big white shingle — There it is. Myron Madchen, MD.'

Parker looked and saw another two-story building, like most of them along here, with a store downstairs and either offices or residences above. This one had a florist below, venetian blinds over the windows upstairs, and that rectangular white sign with black lettering suspended out over the door beyond the florist's window. He said, 'We're meeting at a doctor's office?'

'Beckham's idea,' Dalesia said, pulling into a parking place a few doors farther on. 'I like it.'

They got out of the Audi, and as they walked back along the empty sidewalk, Dalesia said, 'I heard of guys doing this with lawyers before, meet at his office because the law can't bug a lawyer's office because of lawyer-client privilege, but it works just as good with a doctor. Patient confidentiality. It could be even better, because lawyers worry about the law all the time, but what doctors worry about is money.'

Dalesia opened the door beneath the doctor's sign, which had another, more discreet sign in its curtained window, and Parker followed him up a steep carpeted staircase with oak railings on both sides. At the top were two dark-stained wooden doors, both with brass plaques screwed to them. The one straight ahead read PRIVATE and the one to the right read ENTER.

Dalesia pushed open ENTER and they stepped into a large square waiting room with shabby armchairs and worn carpet. Three people who looked like the room were waiting there; all looked up from their magazines, then down again.

Across the way was a glassless window in the opposite wall, and beyond that a smaller office with a woman seated at a desk, behind her a row of white filing cabinets. Dalesia crossed to the window, Parker following, and said to the woman, 'Turner, I got an appointment.'

'William Turner? Yes, here you are. Has the doctor seen you before?'

'Oh, sure, I'm in your files.' Jabbing a thumb at Parker, he said, 'This is Dr Harris, my diagnostician.'

This didn't seem to surprise the woman at all. Making a note, she said, 'Just have a seat, the doctor will see you shortly.'

'Thanks.'

They found adjoining chairs in front of the venetian-blinded windows, and leafed through fairly elderly newsmagazines. After about three minutes, the woman behind the window said, 'Mrs Hancock,' and one of the waiting patients got up and went through the interior door.

Parker said, 'Lawyers are quicker.'

Dalesia thought that was funny. 'Yeah, they are.'

Two or three minutes later, a man who must be the doctor himself came out the door that Mrs Hancock had gone in. He was a heavyset, polished-looking man of about fifty, with lush iron-gray hair combed straight back over a high forehead, and large, pale eyeglasses that bounced the light. He carried a manila folder, and his eyes swept casually over Parker and Dalesia as he walked to the open window, bent there, and spoke briefly with the woman. He gave her the manila folder, turned away, scanned Parker and Dalesia again, and went back into his office.

Now it was less than a minute before the woman said, 'Mr Turner.'

Dalesia got to his feet. 'Yeah?'

'Go right in.'

Dalesia and Parker stepped through the interior door to a narrow fluorescent-lit hallway with closed doors along both sides. A shy girl dressed as a nurse smiled at them and opened a door on the right, saying, 'Just in here. Dr Madchen will be right with you.'

'Thanks,' Dalesia said.

They went through, and she closed the door after them. This was an examination room, with a long examining table and two chrome-and-green vinyl chairs. The walls were covered with glass-fronted cabinets of medical supplies, and posters about various diseases.

Seated on the examining table, reading a *People* magazine while his feet dangled above the floor, was a stocky fiftyish man in an open gray zippered wind-breaker and shapeless cotton chinos. He looked like a carny roustabout who didn't realize he was too old to run away with the circus.

When Parker and Dalesia came in, he tossed the magazine onto the table, hopped to his feet, and stuck his hand out in Dalesia's direction, saying, 'Whadaya say, Nick?'

'Nice place you got here,' Dalesia said, shaking hands.

The man laughed and put his hand out toward Parker, saying, 'You'd be Parker, I guess. I'm Jake Beckham.'

Taking the hand, finding it strong but not insistent, Parker said, 'This is an examining room.'

'That's what it is, all right,' Beckham said. He was proud of his meeting place.

Parker said, 'So why don't we all look at our chests?'

Surprised, Beckham laughed and said, 'By God, you're right! Nick, this guy is good.'

They all stripped to the waist, showing that none of them carried a recorder or transmitter. Dressing again, Beckham said to Parker, 'Nick told you the idea, I guess.'

'Two banks merge, move the goods from one to the other. You've got an inside woman to tell you which truck the cash is in.'

'And some inside woman she is,' Beckham said, grinning to let them know he'd slept with her. 'Sit down, guys, let me tell you the situation.'

While the other two took the vinyl chairs, Beckham hopped back up on the examination table. He was a bulky guy, but he moved as though he thought he was a skinny kid. Settled, he said, 'Small banks are getting eat up, all around the country. If they don't bulk up by merging with one another, they get swallowed by some international monster out of London or Hong Kong. The bank in this town — you might've noticed it, coming in: very old-fashioned, brick, with a clock tower — it's called Rutherford Combined Savings, and the 'Combined' means it already ate a couple even smaller banks, outfits with three offices in three towns ten miles apart. So now Rutherford's got maybe twenty branches all around the western half of the state, and a little farther south you've got Deer Hill Bank, four branches. Deer Hill's who I used to work for before they caught me with my hand in the till.'

Parker said, 'Nick says you did time.'

'Seven to ten, served three. Well, two years, eleven months, four days.' With the boyish grin that seemed strange on that heavy face, he said, 'You know yourself, there's some things you don't round off.'

'No.'

'My history is simple,' Beckham said, 'but I guess you oughta know it. Into the army at

21

eighteen, they made me an MP, based in Germany for a while, saw how an MP could supplement his income. But I didn't really like the army, so after a couple close calls — I never did get caught at anything, but I got suspected a lot — after a couple of those, end of my second enlistment, I quit. Seemed to make sense to go into policing, so I did. Not big towns — I don't want to spend my life doing shootouts with drug dealers — small cities like this. But I think my army years made me a little too rough-and-ready for those civilians, so after a while I didn't have any more police jobs, and that's when I went to work doing security for Deer Hill. The president was a hard-drinking old guy named Lefcourt, Harvey Lefcourt, and him and me got along just fine. Harvey's daughter Elaine was married to a smarmy piece of shit named Jack Langen, and Harvey was bringing him into the business, vice president and all, because on his own Jack Langen would starve to death in a supermarket and take Elaine down with him. So I was in charge of security, I hired and fired the guards, hired the companies that maintained the vaults and the deposit boxes, did all of that, found some ways to dip in here and there, but I'm afraid I wasn't as smart as I thought I was.'

Beckham grinned and shook his head. He

seemed mostly amused at himself, as though he were observing his own raffish kid brother and not himself. He said, 'An audit found my footprints, followed them to me. Harvey didn't want to prosecute, he'd of just let me go without a recommendation, but Jack Langen pressed it all the way. I don't think he knew I was putting it to his wife, I think it was just the natural evil of a useless piece of shit handed a little authority. So in I went, and two years, eleven months, four days later out I got, and called Elaine, and we went back to seeing each other from time to time while I took a crap assistant manager job at a motel down by the MassPike. Harvey had died while I was inside and pissant Jack Langen was the president now, and when Rutherford Combined come along he was more than happy to sell out to them for lowball dollar and a make-work place on their board. Deer Hill doesn't even get to keep its name, it just becomes part of the Combined.'

Parker said, 'This doesn't sit well with the wife.'

'With the *daughter*,' Beckham said. 'She's more Harvey's daughter than she is Jack Langen's wife. I think she'd have left him long ago except he had the bank, and the bank, as far as she was concerned, was Harvey. So she stuck around to watch out for the company the way Harvey would, and if he was alive Harvey would rather get swallowed up by some Chink from Hong Kong than the tight-asses of Rutherford Combined, that's how Elaine sees it, and I think she's right. So once Deer Hill is gone, she'll be gone, too. Not with me, she's got more sense than that, but gone somewhere she can do some good for herself. And for that, she'll need money. She wouldn't wind up very far ahead just divorcing Jack Langen, she knows what he's like, so what the hell. She called me, we did some pillow talk, and the idea was, I put a string together and take Deer Hill's cash and give her a third. That way, she screws Jack Langen *and* Rutherford Combined, and she can still divorce the weasel and get on with her life. And two-thirds of Deer Hill's bank money would be a very comfortable amount for us boys.'

Beckham looked around at them, bright-eyed, pleased with himself. 'Well, Mr Parker,' he said. 'What do you think?'

5

'I don't like it,' Parker said.

Surprised, Beckham said, 'You don't? What's wrong with it?'

'Most things,' Parker told him. 'The hinge of the thing is an amateur. Even a calm amateur is usually trouble, and this one is all emotion. It isn't about money, it's about revenge and anger and family pride. I can't use any of those things.'

'No, you're right,' Beckham said. He had nodded all the way through Parker's statement, and now he nodded another minute more, as though mulling over in his mind the rightness of what Parker had said. Finished nodding, he said, 'It may be I'm kidding myself, I hope not. It may be you can talk me out of a big mistake that'd put me right back inside, where I do not want to be. Because you're right about the whole thing, Elaine is one pissed-off lady, and if I'm just some pussy-whipped clown she's using to get revenge on her husband then I oughta be told about it by somebody before I do myself an injury.' He shook his head and turned to Dalesia to say, 'The reason I went up last time, I wasn't careful enough, didn't take everything into consideration. Am I doing that again? I sure hope not.'

'Well, Jake,' Dalesia said, 'so far, it sounds to me as though maybe that's what's happening.'

'Shit,' said Beckham. 'Mr Parker, let me try something here. Let me walk you through it the way I see it, how the details go down, and you tell me if there's any more sense in it once you know what I have in mind. If you still say it's no good, I'm gonna have to rethink here, and I'll tell you the truth, I don't have a plan B.'

Parker said, 'How long can we stay in this room?'

'This won't take long. Honest.'

Parker shrugged. 'Go ahead, then.'

'The first thing you have to know,' Beckham told him, 'is that Elaine isn't any part of it. Not what we're doing. The bank is gonna make this move, close down the Deer Hill office, no sooner than two weeks from now and no later than the first of November, because they don't want to get all mixed up with weather and skiers. It all depends on weather, and when the armored cars and the private security are available. They won't know for sure until about five days before they make the move. As soon as Elaine finds out through her husband when that will be, and which car the cash will be in, she'll get word to me, and that's the last she has to do with anything. I already know the route, so that's taken care of. The night comes, we make our move, we disappear.'

'Well, *you* don't disappear,' Parker told him. 'You're on parole, aren't you?'

'And I'm being a very good boy, believe me. And Dr Madchen is gonna see to it I'm in the hospital that night, I'm gonna come down with something not too serious. He'll put me in a private room, so I can sneak out of there to do the job and then back, and that's my alibi.'

Parker and Dalesia looked at each other, expressionless. Then Parker said, 'Beckham, what's this Dr Madchen to you?'

'There's a cousin of his,' Beckham said, 'got into drugs, wound up in the same can as me. I knew the doctor from before, you know, just as a patient, and he wrote to me, asked me to help with his cousin, he was afraid the cousin wasn't up to taking care of himself on the inside, and let me tell you, was he ever right. So I did help, and took care of the guy, and now the good doctor feels he owes me one, and this is it.' Beckham grinned again, in that boyish way that seemed so at odds with who he was. 'So there you are,' he said.

'There's my alibi. I'm in the hospital when it happens, I couldn't be involved.'

Parker shook his head. 'No,' he said.

Now Beckham looked more frustrated than worried. 'Still no? Why? I've got the emotional one out of it, I've got my own alibi, you guys are big boys and can take care of yourselves, work out your own cover. The job is *good*, Mr Parker, I know it is, that target is good, that armored car full of cash.'

'Yes, it is,' Parker agreed. 'That part is all right, that's what got me here. If it was just that, we could do it and no problem.'

'You still see problems,' Beckham said.

'Two, to start with,' Parker said. 'In the first place, it'll take the cops about twenty minutes to work out the link between you and the doctor.'

Beckham looked bewildered. 'Why are they gonna look?'

'Because you're the one they're going to want for the job, from the start,' Parker told him. 'The minute it happens, they're going to be looking for you, and there you are in a hospital. Hospital? Who put you in this hospital? What's the connection between you and this doctor? If another doctor looks you over, because the police want to know what the story is here, what's he gonna find?'

Beckham shook his head, a man bedeviled

by gnats. 'But why are they gonna just think about *me?*'

Dalesia said, 'Let me tell him that part.'

'Go ahead,' Parker said.

Dalesia said to Beckham, 'Parker's right, the job's all clouded up because of emotions. Including yours, Jake.'

Beckham reared back on the examination table, his feet floating above the floor. Clutching at his chest, he said, 'Mine?'

Dalesia said, 'The husband — What's his name?'

'Jack Langen, the little prick.'

'There you go,' Dalesia said. 'You just said it yourself.'

Beckham spread his hands. 'Said what?'

'Jack Langen isn't the little prick,' Dalesia told him. 'He's the angry husband. He knew you were putting it to his wife from the very first.'

'He doesn't know his ass — '

'*That's* why he pressed charges on you the first time,' Dalesia told him. 'Overrode his father-in-law, put it to you because he knew you were putting it to the missus. And the minute you got out, he knew when it started up again. Part of this bank merger deal is to get back at the wife and not be the young nobody brought into the family business any more.'

Parker said, 'And the second this job goes down, he'll know it's you, with her help. He'll right away start saying your name to the cops, and telling them why it has to be you, and why his own wife has to be the insider. You're all they'll look at, and that's why they'll see through the doctor alibi in a heartbeat.'

Dalesia said, 'Jake, all you wanted was to feel contempt for the husband, like he didn't matter, like you were that much smarter than him. That's called underestimating your enemy, Jake.'

'Shit,' Beckham said. 'You mean, it still can't be done?' Turning to Parker, he said, 'You said yourself, without the emotions in it the job is good. I really want to do this, Mr Parker, I need the stake, I need to get my life together. Do you see any way at all we could still pull it off?'

'One way,' Parker said. 'I was thinking about it while Nick was telling you things. There's one way you *might* get the cops to stop looking at you.'

'I'll do it,' Beckham said.

'We'll see.'

'Why?' Beckham looked a little alarmed. 'What do you want me to do?'

'Violate parole,' Parker said.

6

'Violate — ' Beckham stared at Dalesia, then at Parker: 'What are you talking about?'

'How often you have to report in?'

'Twice a month. But I don't see — '

'When's your next time?'

'Next Tuesday,' Beckham said. 'Ten in the morning. But — '

'You don't show up,' Parker said. 'What you do — '

'The hell I don't show up!' Beckham was so agitated he actually hopped off the examination table and stood with one hand pressed on the table behind him. He wasn't angry; he was just staggered by the idea. 'The whole thing I been doing since I got out,' he said, 'is build a record, no violations. Same as when I was in, got full good-behavior time credit.'

Dalesia said, 'Listen to him, Jake.'

Beckham didn't want to. He shook his head, then folded his arms and glowered at Parker, waiting.

'What you do,' Parker told him, 'the day you're supposed to report, you fly to Vegas. That's Tuesday. Saturday, you turn yourself in to the Vegas cops, you're a parole violator, you don't know what came over you, met a woman, got drunk, flew away with her, you know you're in trouble, nothing like this ever happened before, you just want to get straight with the law.'

'They'll lock me up,' Beckham said.

'Yes, they will,' Parker said. 'By the time they check you out, do a hearing there, bring you back, give you a hearing here, decide what to do with you, it's three weeks. If the bank move has gone down by then, you get a lawyer, you talk about your good record inside and since, you work your ass off to get time served. If it didn't go down yet, you're sullen, you don't want anybody's help, you'll get another thirty days tacked on.'

'Thanks a lot,' Beckham said.

Dalesia said, 'Jake, don't you get it? You couldn't have had anything to do with the bank job because you were in jail, you were in a cell, the *law* had you.'

'You were already in a cell,' Parker pointed out, 'before you could have known anything about the details of the bank move.'

'But I gotta be there to *do* it,' Beckham said. 'What good is that, I'm in some jail cell? I'm in some jail cell, the job doesn't happen.'

'We do it,' Dalesia said.

Beckham frowned at Dalesia. The idea had

never occurred to him. He said, 'You do it without me?'

'You're still part of it,' Parker assured him. 'You brought it to us, so you're still in it, you get your share. But the law isn't looking at you.'

'Jake,' Dalesia said, 'what Parker's doing, he's getting *all* the emotion out of it, including you. So it's just us, and anybody else we have to bring in.'

'But — ' Beckham couldn't get his mind around this idea. 'I have to be there,' he said. 'When it happens, it's my — I have to be there.'

'If you're there,' Parker told him, 'you're in jail the next day, you and your lady friend both, in different jails, for the next twenty years.'

'If you're *not* there,' Dalesia said, 'if you're already in jail then for some other reason, that's it, you're never behind bars again, you've got your stake, you wait out your parole, the world is yours.'

Parker said, 'Do you want the score, or do you want to make a point? Tell the world off, and go down in flames.'

'Jesus.' Beckham didn't sit on the examination table again, but he leaned backward against it, brow furrowed like corduroy as he stared at the floor, trying to work out this new situation. 'You're asking me . . . ' he decided, and trailed off.

Dalesia picked up on that. 'What, to trust us? You'd never find Parker, Jake, but I couldn't hide from you. We go back a long way. You never wondered about me before. We've been in tents by trout streams up above Quebec, Jake, and we both slept like babies.'

'I know that,' Beckham said, and roused himself. 'Jesus, I don't mistrust you, Nick, and if you say you don't worry about Parker, I won't worry about Parker. But this was *my* baby, it's been my baby from the beginning. It's not like I go off with Elaine at the end of it, what I get is the cash, but it's *my* cash, my score.'

Dalesia said, 'It just happens, Jake, in your score this time, you put the two of us on the send, we come back with the winnings. Meantime, you cover your ass.'

Beckham sighed. 'I gotta get used to this,' he said. 'All right, if this is what has to happen, what do you want from me?'

Dalesia turned to Parker, who said, 'What does Elaine drive?'

'A white Infiniti.'

Dalesia laughed: 'So the marriage isn't *all* downside.'

Beckham showed him a sour face. 'The

car's leased by the bank,' he said. 'It's all scam. She doesn't get to choose it, and she doesn't get to keep it.'

Parker said, 'Do you have a place to stash the money car, once you've got it?'

'Yeah, a good one.' The idea made Beckham smile. 'It's one of those old nineteenth-century factory buildings, old brick, concrete floors, the jobs moved to the South seventy years ago, abandoned ever since, take it a thousand years to rot away.'

'All right.' Parker turned to Dalesia. 'You got anything to do between now and tomorrow?'

'Only this.'

To Beckham, Parker said, 'Tomorrow morning at ten, she drives the Infiniti to the service area on the MassPike west of Huntington. Eastbound side. She parks there, and we'll find her.'

Dalesia said, 'You better tell her what we look like.'

'I don't know,' Beckham said. 'You're bringing her *in*?'

'She brought herself in,' Parker said, 'and you brought her in. She meets with us, she has a map of the money route, she tells us what she knows about which armored car we want, and we give her a phone number to call when she's got the date it's going down. Then she leaves again. The only thing left for her to do, when the move is scheduled, she calls that number. Then maybe she should go shopping in New York for a few days.'

'She does those to Boston,' Beckham said, 'on account of I can't leave the state.'

Dalesia laughed. 'Funny thing is,' he said, 'on the day the job goes down, you *really* won't be able to leave the state.'

7

The old empty factory Beckham had described was in a remnant of a town ten miles south of Rutherford, on a narrow, hilly road that was itself a branch off a secondary road. Down below them to their left, through pine trees, was a fast, twisty stream that the road followed.

As they drove, Dalesia said, 'Jake's problem is, he's still part amateur himself.'

'He is,' Parker said.

'I like him, don't get me wrong, but he didn't start out to be one of us. He started out to be a soldier boy, obey orders, get drunk, chase girls. He got turned and turned, and he's with us now because he's got no place else to be.'

'He brings us a job,' Parker said, without emphasis, 'he got from the woman he's in bed with.'

'I know. It's worse than a soap opera. Do you think you got him to back out of this?'

'Maybe. If not,' Parker said, 'you're the one he can finger.'

Dalesia laughed, but then he said, 'No. I put one in his head before that.'

'Then her head, too.'

Dalesia, considering, said, 'You think so?'

'Never trust pillow talk.'

Dalesia thought about that for a while, then said, 'We could just keep driving.'

'We could.'

'I got nothing else.'

'Neither of us has anything else.'

Dalesia nodded. 'For Jake's sake,' he said, 'I hope he can keep himself under control.'

After a while, the road they were on descended to a flatter, more open area at stream level, and that was where they found the town, or what was left of it: a few old wooden houses with junked cars around them and clothes drying on lines extended back toward the encroaching pines. There were no stores or other commercial establishments.

Then the road made a left turn over a small concrete bridge, with just beyond it the hulk of the factory building on the right and an abandoned old wooden hotel and bar on the left; even the For Sale sign on the hotel had an antique look.

Dalesia turned right onto the weedy gravel on the far side of the factory and stopped at a sagging, rusty chain-link fence. They sat in the Audi a minute, looking out at the brick hulk, and Dalesia said, 'To get here, you gotta go past those houses back there. On this road, at night, you don't do that without lights.'

'Those people don't call the law,' Parker said.

Dalesia thought that over, then nodded and said, 'You're right. Also, we can see where this road goes next. You want a look at the place?'

It was seven in the evening now, twilight just setting in, but still bright enough to see. Parker considered the dark hulk of the factory building, then shook his head. 'I take Beckham's word for it.'

'Me, too.'

They drove on, and after another four and a half miles they came to a numbered county road. There had been no more occupied buildings since the town.

'So what we do,' Dalesia said as they turned south, 'we bring the armored car in from the other way, because that's where their route is between the banks, but the vehicles to take things out again come this way.'

'Stashed ahead of time,' Parker said. 'Right. It's just the one trip that night.'

They drove south a while in silence, toward the general area of the MassPike, and then Dalesia said, 'If it's just you and me and the armored cars and the state cops and the private security, we'll be fine.'

'That's right,' Parker said.

8

They chose a motel that was not the one where Beckham worked these days, and in the morning they checked out and went back to where Parker had left his car. Dalesia put the Audi near it and went on into the restaurant to find a booth, while Parker leaned against the driver's door of his Lexus to wait for Elaine Langen.

At ten in the morning, the parking area was nearly empty — too late for breakfast and too early for lunch; everybody was on the road. Except for the truckers, who had their own parking area around to the side of the building. As Parker waited, a thin but steady trickle of semis arrived and departed, snorting in and groaning out.

She was a few minutes late, which was to be expected, but when she arrived, the white Infiniti would have stood out even if the lot had been full. Watching her roll tentatively down the lane, looking at him but not yet sure he was the right one, Parker nodded first at her, then at the restaurant, then turned to walk indoors.

The interior was cafeteria style, with a mix

of free-standing tables and booths along the windowed walls. Truckers and a few civilians ate at widely scattered tables. Dalesia had taken a booth near the back, beyond the windows. Parker walked toward him and saw Dalesia's expression change, meaning she'd followed him in.

Dalesia was on the side of the booth that faced the front and the entrance, so that whoever sat on the other side would be invisible from most parts of the restaurant. Parker slid in next to him and only then looked toward Elaine Langen.

Well. The first impression was of a slender, stylish, well-put-together woman in her forties, but almost instantly the impression changed. She wasn't slender; she was bone thin, and inside the stylish clothes she walked with a graceless jitteriness, like someone whose medicine had been cut off too soon. Beneath the neat cowl of well-groomed ash-blond hair, her face was too thin, too sharp-featured, too deeply lined. This could have made her look haggard; instead, it made her look mean. From the evidence, what would have attracted her husband most would have been her father's bank.

She walked directly to the table, looked at them both, and said, 'Say a name.'

'Jake Beckham,' Parker said. 'Elaine Langen.'

'That's me.'

'Sit down.'

She looked at the booth, looked at the privacy they'd arranged for her, and said, 'Thank you.' She slid in and said, 'Jake had to talk me into this, you know.'

Dalesia said, 'Into *this*, or into the whole thing?'

Her laugh was brief and harsh. 'Into *this*,' she said. 'I had to talk *him* into the whole thing. But I guess you two must agree with me.'

Parker said, 'About what?'

'There was an old movie,' she said, 'called, *Nice Little Bank That Should Be Robbed.*'

Dalesia laughed and said, 'That's what we've got here, huh? In the movie, did they get away with it?'

'I never saw the movie,' she said. 'I just noticed the title, in a TV listing. It struck me.'

'Probably,' Dalesia said, 'being a movie, they didn't get away with it. Movies are very unrealistic that way.'

She seemed amused by him. 'Oh? Do bank robbers usually get away with it?'

'They *always* get away with it,' Dalesia told her. 'What orders do the bosses give the tellers in *your* bank? 'If they show the note, give them the money. If you can slip them a dye pack, good, but if not, just give them the money.' Less hassle for everybody, right?'

'That's right,' she said. 'But still, they do get caught sometimes.'

'The really stupid ones,' he agreed. 'Also, if you do it a hundred twenty-two times, the hundred twenty-third they're gonna grab you. Everybody's gotta show a little restraint.'

She considered him. 'What number are you up to?'

'One.'

Parker said, 'You've got a map for us.'

A little surprised, she gave Parker an appraising look, then looked again at Dalesia. 'Well, it isn't exactly good cop, bad cop,' she said, 'but it works the same. Yes,' she told Parker, and reached into the shoulder bag she'd put on the seat beside her.

Parker said, 'You got a gun in there, too?'

Surprised again, she said, 'As a matter of fact, yes. I don't intend to show it.'

'Then don't carry it.'

She had taken from her bag a sheet of typing paper folded in half, but now she paused to say, 'I've taken courses. I know how to fire a weapon, and I know how to hit what I aim at. And I also know never to show it unless I intend to use it. I carry it because I live in an uncertain world.'

'That's true,' Parker said.

She extended the paper toward him. He took it, unfolded it, and it was a Xerox copy of a page from a Massachusetts atlas, in black-and-white, showing one small section of the state in close detail. On it a route had been indicated by a few short lines in red ink. *Deer Hill* was at the southern end of the red line, *Rutherford* at the north. West Ruudskill, the town with Beckham's factory in it, was a dot off the middle of the route, to the right.

Parker folded the map twice and put it in his shirt pocket. She watched him, then said, 'Jake says you're doing it without him, but you'll still share and share alike.' She sounded as though she didn't entirely believe it.

Parker said, 'Did he tell you why he's staying away?'

Dalesia corrected that: 'Why it's *better* for him that he stays away.'

Her mouth, thin to begin with, twisted a little. 'You've got him convinced Jack knows about us.'

'Knew the first round,' Dalesia said, 'knows this round.'

She held a hand up to stop him. 'Don't give me the arguments, please,' she said. 'They're just arguments. You've convinced Jake, that's all that matters, and he's going to do whatever it is you told him to do, but it so happens I know my husband. Jack could not fool me, not for a minute.'

Parker said, 'Beckham didn't tell you what we thought he should do?'

'No.' She shook her head, remembering. 'To tell the truth, he seemed a little embarrassed about it.'

'He is,' Parker said. 'We told him he should violate parole.'

She stared. 'You *what?*'

'That means he's inside,' Dalesia explained, 'from before anybody knows the date of the move. After the job, he comes back out.'

'My God,' she said. 'I know how Jake feels about prison. You really sold him a bill of goods.'

'We showed him what's out there,' Parker said.

She shrugged. 'Well, that's up to him. You're supposed to give me a phone number or something?'

This was Dalesia's part. 'It's a fax number,' he said. 'I think we can be pretty sure the move won't happen until October, that's less than two weeks from now.'

'I think so, too,' she said.

'So when you know the date,' he told her, 'you write just that, the day, seven or fifteen or whatever — '

'I get the idea.'

'You write just that on a piece of paper,' he

said, 'and fax it to this number. It's somebody I know that's not gonna ask me what it's about. All I want you to do, get rid of the fax number afterwards.'

'I assume,' she said, 'it's a long-distance call. It will be on my bill.'

Parker said, 'There are fax machines in your bank branches.'

Surprised, she said, 'That's true. All right, I can do it.'

Dalesia already had the number on a small slip of paper in his pocket. He handed it to her and said, 'Don't copy it anywhere.'

'Don't insult me any more,' she said, and put the paper in her bag.

'Sorry,' Dalesia said.

Parker said, 'You were gonna tell us about the armored cars.'

'Four of them. They'll be coming that day from Boston,' she said. 'There'll be rooms for the drivers at the Green Man Motel outside Deer Hill for that night. They'll get some sleep, then get up and get to the bank at one-thirty to start the move. We'll have people from a moving company to do the heavy lifting. One decision that's been made for sure is that the car with the cash will not be the first or the fourth, so it'll be one of the two in the middle.'

Parker said, 'When do you know which?'

'When they start to load.'

Parker shook his head. 'That's no good. The idea was, we'd know which armored car of the four, not which two of the four.'

Sounding dubious, she said, 'I could fax that number, I suppose, that night, a two or a three.'

'Too late,' Dalesia said.

Parker said, 'Are you going to be there, to watch the move?'

'For a while, at the start,' she said. 'It's interesting, it's kind of fascinating, to make a move like that. But I don't intend to stay up all night.'

Parker said, 'You'll leave before they finish loading.'

'That's what I plan to do, yes.'

He took out of his pocket the map she'd given him, unfolded it onto the table. 'Which way do you drive, to go home?'

'The same route, really, most of the way. I turn west before Rutherford, on Route Twenty-seven. It's a little county road.'

'I see it,' Parker said, tracing the road with his finger. 'Where do you meet a stop sign on that road?'

Again she made her bitter, unamused laugh. 'Everywhere. I hit four of them on the way home.'

'How about Route Thirty-two here?'

'That's one of them.'

'What time do you want to get there? One-thirty? Two?'

'No later than two. But you know, they'll still be loading, back at the bank. I might not know whether it's going to be the second or the third when they leave.'

'Those armored cars,' Parker told her, 'are part of a fleet. They'll have their own numbers on them. By the time you leave, you'll know which one is getting the cash. You write the fleet number of that car on a piece of paper, you get to that intersection at two o'clock, and when you stop there a car will come the other way, with one of us in it. We stop, you hand the paper over, you drive home. Will your husband still be at the bank?'

'Until the bitter end, absolutely.'

'Then, when you get home, you phone him. He knows what time you left, he knows what time you got home, he knows you didn't have time to stop and talk to anybody.'

Frowning, she said, 'You really believe it, don't you? That Jack will suspect *me*.'

'Whether he does or not,' Parker said, 'do you like to take risks?'

'To wind up in jail, you mean?' Her mouth twisted again. 'Prison orange is not my color.'

'You'll stop at the stop sign at two, you'll call your husband when you get home.'

Dalesia said, 'Just call us worrywarts.'

She looked at him, and could be seen to relax, just a bit. 'Good cop, bad cop,' she said, and looked at Parker again. 'Is there anything else?'

'No. We won't see you again, except at the stop sign. Now, you want to leave here before we do; we'll give you a few minutes.'

'Good.' She gathered up her bag, but paused before she got out of the booth. 'You didn't even buy me a cup of coffee,' she said, then rose, and walked away.

9

In this part of New Jersey, three hours south of Massachusetts, the September days were sometimes summer, sometimes fall. This was one of the summer days. Parker thumbed the garage opener on the Lexus visor and drove, in from bright afternoon sunlight to the cool, dim interior. As the garage door noisily slid downward again, he got out of the car and went through the door into the kitchen, then on into the living room. Looking out past the screened porch toward the lake, he saw Claire swimming strongly back and forth out there beyond the boathouse. A little later in the season, after the summer people had closed up their 'cottages' for the year, leaving only a fifth of the houses around the lake occupied, and on those rare autumnal days of strong sun, it would be possible to swim nude, but in mid-September half the houses were still in use, so as Claire swam, Parker caught glimpses of a bright blue two-piece suit.

He carried his bag to the bedroom, changed into his own swimsuit, and went out to the lake. She saw him and smiled and lifted an arm in greeting, but didn't break off from the rhythm of her movements; she was doing laps, competing with herself.

Parker dove in from the end of their concrete dock and swam beside her a while, working his muscles. The long hours in the car had left him stiff, too aware of his body.

The water was cold and clear and slid over the skin like velvet. If you put your head beneath the surface, you could see the muddy bottom, quickly sloping away toward the deep middle. If you looked around, there was no one else on the lake, either swimming or boating.

This was the earliest in the year they would ever occupy their house. From Memorial Day till Labor Day, when the summer people were here, running their motorboats and their barbeque parties, Parker and Claire traveled. Without a passport, he couldn't leave the country, except occasionally to Canada or Mexico, but they found places to interest them.

The best times here at the house were in the depths of winter, with the lake frozen solid enough to drive a car on, and no other lights to be seen anywhere around the nine-mile perimeter of the shore after the brief twilight was done. But this now in mid-September was all right, too, when swimming and privacy both were possible.

Neither spoke till Claire was finished counting her laps and they paddled together to the dock. Then, climbing out, she said, 'Was everything all right?'

'So far.'

They toweled themselves, moving toward the house and the bedroom. She said, 'When do you go again?'

'They'll call me.'

'Good,' she said. 'You'll be here a while.'

★ ★ ★

It wasn't really cool enough for a fire that night, but Claire liked the look of it, so after dinner she laid one as he made drinks. He brought them to the living room and they offered one another a silent toast. They were both in their dark satin robes, which gleamed dully in the firelight.

They sat a while on the side sofa, where they could see the red-black of the fireplace to their left and the white-black of the moonlit lake to the right. An open window competed with the fire, and the night sounds of insects competed with the crackle of the burning wood.

He told her about Elaine Langen, and Claire said, 'She's unhappy.'

'She could have folded the hand.'

'No, I mean, if she's unhappy, you don't know who she's going to take it out on.'

'We're keeping her at a distance.'

'Good.'

He said, 'How about here? Everything all right?'

'The checking account is getting low.'

'I'll get some cash, later on.'

★   ★   ★

When Parker scored, he stashed part of it away for use later, when needed. At times like this, when he hadn't earned for a while, he would visit one of those stashes.

They were handy, but they were not in the house. At one-thirty that morning, in black polo shirt, chinos, and rubber-soled black deck shoes, he left the darkened house and went out the driveway to the road that circled the lake. Turning left, he walked in the darkness past houses already boarded up for the winter and others that would still be occupied for a few more weekends. There were no streetlights out here, nor could he see any other light.

The residents of several of these houses would never know that thousands of dollars in cash were salted within, behind paneling or under floors. If there were a few of these stashes he didn't get around to reclaiming, somebody doing new construction work years from now would be in for a happy surprise.

The house he chose tonight, a broad black shape against the moon-reflecting lake, was empty but not yet closed up for the season. He'd arranged simple entry for his storage houses, and didn't need light for what he was doing. When he came back out, the four Ziploc bags beneath his shirt contained five thousand dollars in cash each. Claire could deposit it, three and four thousand at a time, in the checking account she used to keep this place going. He didn't use it; he didn't sign checks.

★　★　★

The next Tuesday afternoon, Parker was seated in a chaise on the deck, in the sunshine, thinking about nothing, when he heard the phone ring in the house. He stood, and was halfway across the lawn when Claire came out, the cordless phone in her hand. 'Nick,' she said, with a rising inflection: Did he want to be home?

'That's good,' he said, and reached for the phone.

As she handed it over, she said, 'Does this mean you're going now?'

'Not yet.'

But when he spoke into the phone, Dalesia's voice said, 'A glitch.'

'What kind?'

'Jake was a good boy. He kept his parole appointment.'

10

This time there was no nonsense about doctors' offices. Dalesia knew that Beckham lived in a mobile home park near the motel where he worked, so they drove there, this time in a Saab from the long-term parking at Bradley International Airport, north of Hartford, less than an hour away.

They pulled in at the parking lot in front of the mobile home park office just as twilight was settling in. Behind a large wooden sign reading *Riviera Park* were several rows of mobile homes in pastels and silver and white, like a cross between a lineup of Monopoly houses and a display of beehives. The office itself was a similar structure, but smaller and simpler; if it still had its wheels instead of those concrete blocks, it would be called a trailer.

They went into the former trailer through the metal-and-glass door under the red neon OFFICE sign, and a very old and very wiry woman in jeans and gray sweatshirt looked up from the crossword puzzle book she had spread open on her counter, to say, 'I hope you fellas aren't lookin for a place to park. I'm full up.'

Dalesia said, 'An old pal of ours is a tenant of yours. We thought we'd come by and say hello.'

She put down her pen and straightened up. 'Who would he be?'

'Jake Beckham.'

She smiled, pleased at the name. 'Oh, Jake! Very nice fella.'

'Sure is,' Dalesia said. 'We know he works over at that motel, so we didn't know if we should look for him here or there. What is it now?' He looked up at the round clock on the wall above and behind her. 'Almost seven-thirty. I think he works days, doesn't he?'

'Lemme call him,' she said, 'see is he in.'

'Thanks.'

She had to look up the number in a ledger book from under the counter, then dialed it, listened, and perked up when she said, 'Oh, Jake! There's a couple fellas here for you.'

Dalesia said, 'Tell him it's Nick.'

'He says it's Nick.'

Dalesia said, 'Could I talk to him?'

'Hold on, Jake, he wants to talk to you.'

Dalesia, full of good-fellowship, said into the phone, 'Whadaya say, Jake? We're in the neighborhood, we thought we'd come by, say hello. If this isn't a bad time? Great. Nah, we'll come back to you, we're just driving through. See you in a minute.' Handing the phone back to the woman, he said, 'Thanks.'

'Any time.' She put the phone away and said, 'You can't drive back there, though, we don't have room for cars inside. Even the residents, they park out here and walk in. Some keep little wagons behind here to carry their groceries.'

'We don't mind walking,' Dalesia assured her.

She turned and pointed at the wall behind her. 'You go out there and walk straight, you're on Cans Way. First you cross is San Tropays Lane and the next is Nice Lane.' She pronounced it like 'a nice day.' 'Nice Lane is what you want,' she said. 'Go down there to the right, Jake's house is second on your left, a very nice pea-green.'

'Thank you,' Dalesia said, and they went back out the door they'd come in, around to the back of the onetime trailer, past a bunch of rusty red wagons chained to a long iron bar fastened to concrete blocks in the ground, and past an ordinary street sign, white letters on green, reading *Cannes Way*.

The road was not much wider than the mobile homes parked to both sides. Dalesia said, 'They must get themselves a river pilot to bring these things in and out.'

'Maybe so.'

'Or airlift them.'

They passed a cross street signed *St Tropez Way*, then turned right on *Nice Lane*, and there was Jake Beckham waiting for them, standing in the open doorway of his pea-green mobile home.

'I know what you're gonna say,' he said as they approached. 'And don't say it.'

Dalesia went on inside, but Parker stopped in the doorway, looked at Beckham, and said, 'I was going to say, the job works just as good with you dead.'

Beckham blinked, and Parker walked past him into a long, narrow living room with dark paneled walls and, on the small windows, red and white checked curtains like tablecloths in a French restaurant.

Dalesia had gone off to the right, to look in the bathroom and both bedrooms, while Parker turned left, to look at an empty small galley kitchen, the brushed-chrome built-ins neat but the dirty dishes piled on them not.

Dalesia and Parker both returned to the living room, shook their heads, and turned to Beckham, who had shut the door and stood with his back to it, warily watching them. Parker said, 'Tell us about it.'

'You didn't have to say that,' Beckham told him. The usual boyishness that was such a misfit on him had been rattled now. He was acting his age. 'That was unnecessary,' he said, 'you didn't have to say it.'

'So far,' Parker told him, 'you're putting yourself at risk, and you're putting the job at risk. Is there any way you can put *me* at risk? I don't think so, but now I'll wait and see.'

Pursuing his own thought, Beckham said, 'And it isn't even true, what you said. You don't need me? Of course you need me. If I'm dead, Elaine gives you nothing. If Elaine doesn't give, what've you got?'

'Jake,' Dalesia said, sounding sad for his friend, 'what Parker was saying was, you disappointed us. You disappointed *me*, Jake, and I'm the one told Parker you were all right, the job was all right. He counted on me, Jake, and I counted on you.'

'It's all figured out,' Beckham said. Still with wary looks toward Parker, he took a step into the room. 'Why don't we all sit down?' he suggested, and fluttered a hand at the plaid-and-maple furniture.

'Not yet,' Parker said. 'It was all figured out that you had to take yourself out of the job in a way the law would believe, or they'd be all over you and then all over our backtrail. That was what was figured out.'

'It still is,' Beckham insisted. 'Dr Madchen — '

Exasperated, Dalesia said, 'Back with *that*, Jake? We already know that doesn't work.'

'I can't do prison again,' Beckham said. 'I don't care if it's just a county jug somewhere, I can't do it, I can't go back, not again.'

'Then there's no job,' Parker said.

'There *is*. Will you listen to me about the doctor? We worked it out, I went to him, we got it worked out. Jesus Christ, fellas, come on, will ya? Sit down, we'll all sit down, let me tell you what we got, and if you don't like it, you don't like it, but no matter what happens, me being dead doesn't help, you know that.'

'Maybe it relieves our feelings,' Dalesia said, but he sat down, and so did Parker, and then so did Beckham.

Parker said, 'You went back to this doctor.'

'Yeah, I needed something except jail, I needed — '

'What does he know, this doctor?'

Beckham took a deep breath. 'He knows I'm on my way to a score, so then I can retire. He knows the guys he saw in his office are in it.'

'Does he know what the score is?'

'Yes, but he's all right, he isn't a problem for us, he's a help. I'm gonna give him a piece out of my share and you guys don't have to have anything to do with him. And in the meantime, he's solved this problem here.'

Dalesia said, 'How did he solve it, Jake?'

'The first change is,' Beckham said, 'I stay in the hospital.' Now that he was getting to tell his story, the irrepressible kid inside him was beginning to emerge again, giving him more animated gestures. In that chair, his feet touched the floor, but he acted as though they didn't. 'You remember,' he said, 'the original idea was, I was gonna sneak out of this private room, be part of the operation.'

'That was never going to fly,' Parker said.

'OK, I've accepted that,' Beckham said, moving his arms and his shoulders around. 'I'm away from it, but I still get my taste.'

'If you're locked up,' Parker told him, 'as a parole violator.'

'This is just as good,' Beckham insisted. 'See, I go to the doctor about these stomach cramps, he does tests, he can't find the problem, it could be a bunch of things. Believe me, he knows what to put down for the diagnosis.'

'We believe that, Jake.'

'Fine. He puts me in the hospital for tests and observation, I'm going in next Monday, he's doing all the paperwork now, all the stuff to show the law, if anybody comes around — I even told my parole lady about it this morning. See, this was a long-term medical problem, the time was right to put me in the hospital, do the tests. If they don't find anything, fine, it was nerves, still shook up from being inside and then outside. Bring on all your second opinions in the world, nobody's gonna find a thing.'

Dalesia said, 'Parker? What do you think?'

Parker said, 'Beckham, he was your doctor before you went inside, right?'

'Oh, yeah, we already knew each other, I was already his patient.'

'Still a private room?'

'No! An eight-bed ward, man, it's all I can afford with the insurance I get at the motel.'

'You're going in Monday.'

'And today, in fact,' Beckham said, 'the doctor's started making the appointments for me, the date, the bed, the tests. I mean, the alibi's already *started*.'

Dalesia said, 'Parker? OK?'

Parker shrugged. If it was going to happen, this would have to be the way. 'It sounds good,' he said.

'It *is* good,' Beckham insisted.

'And not wanting to go back inside . . . ' Parker spread his hands. 'I can understand that.'

11

When Parker got back to the lake a little before noon the next day, Claire was in the living room, reading a shelter magazine. She tossed it aside, got to her feet, and said, 'Oh, good, I was hoping you'd be home before lunch. Take me someplace nice, with a terrace. There won't be many beautiful days like this left.'

'We can drive over to Pennsylvania,' he said. 'There's some places along the river there.'

She looked doubtful. 'With good food?'

'You want good food *and* a terrace?'

She laughed. 'You're right. Come with me while I look at my hair. We got a very strange wrong number this morning.'

'What kind of strange?' He stood in the bedroom doorway and watched her poke at her trim auburn hair, which had been flawless when she started.

'He asked for somebody called Harbin.'

Harbin was the guy in Cincinnati who'd worn the wire. Parker said, 'Then what?'

'I said wrong number, he said why didn't I ask around the people here, and I said there wasn't anybody to ask, not at the moment. He said he'd call back. There. All right?'

'Perfect,' he said.

★   ★   ★

The guy called again the next day, Thursday. Claire took the call and brought it to Parker, looking at New England maps in the living room. 'It's him again.'

Parker took the phone, and she went away to give him privacy as he said, 'Yeah?'

'I'm looking for Harbin.' The voice was gravelly and a little false; not as though he were trying to sound tougher, but softer.

'Which Harbin would that be?'

'The Harbin from Cincinnati.'

'Don't know the guy, sorry.'

'Well, wait a minute, I think you can help me.'

'I don't.'

'From your phone number, I got a pretty good idea your general geographical location. I can get up into that northwest corner of New Jersey in, say, an hour. Give me directions to your place, we can talk it over.'

'There's nothing to talk about.'

'I just don't want to leave a stone unturned here,' said the gravelly voice, sliding back and forth between menace and gentleness. 'I'm

65

the kind of guy, I'm dogged, I just keep coming.'

'Then I tell you what,' Parker said. 'What kind of car you driving?'

'Oh, you wanna meet somewhere else. Sure, that's OK, I'm in a dark red Chevy Suburban, Illinois plates. What about you?'

'On Route Twenty-four,' Parker told him, 'eleven miles from the Delaware Water Gap, there's a Mobil station, north side of the road. I could be there in two hours.'

'So could I, pal. What kinda car am I looking for?'

'I'll recognize you,' Parker said.

⋆   ⋆   ⋆

Of course he didn't show up, but neither did Parker. The voice had said he could make it to this neighborhood in an hour, so forty-five minutes after the call, Parker took up a position at the diner across the road from the Mobil station and a little farther on toward Pennsylvania. From where he sat, he was unobtrusive, but he could see everything that drove by the Mobil station, and after two hours not one red Chevy Suburban had done so. There were no pedestrians out here along this country road through pine woods, so there was nothing for him to watch for but a car, and none showed up.

Had the guy lied about his car, or was he hanging even farther back somewhere behind Parker or down the other way, eastward, toward New York?

Who had the other people been at that meeting? Parker had never met any of them before except Nick Dalesia. What were their names? Stratton, their host, was the one Dalesia had known, who had invited Dalesia in. McWhitney was the one who'd brought the wired Harbin, but had sworn he hadn't known about it. The other two were Fletcher and Mott.

This gravelly voice on the phone was none of those, but he had to be connected to one of them. At this point, he could represent either side of the law.

But whatever he represented, Parker wanted nothing to do with him and didn't want to have to spend a lot of time on him. This week wasn't so bad, but after this week the bank job could happen on any day. He needed to find out who this guy was, who he was connected to, and what he wanted. And then he needed, one way or another, to make him go away.

Two hours and fifteen minutes outside the diner. It was now three hours since the call. Parker started the Lexus and drove away from there, not seeing any sudden activity in his mirrors.

He drove to the turnoff at the lake road, made the turn, and then drove very slowly, watching the inter-section back there. He was almost around the first curve to the left, which would block the view, when a small black car made the turn into his mirror.

He accelerated around the curve, then slowed again. This road went all the way around the lake, partly straightaways and partly left-leaning curves, and then came back out onto the state highway two miles farther west.

Because he'd accelerated into the curve, then slowed, the small black car was closer when it next appeared, but it immediately braked, its nose dipping, then came on more slowly, trying to hang farther back.

It was the stutter that said this was no civilian. Parker drove on past his own driveway, with the mail-box marked WILLIS, the name Claire used around here. Behind him, the black car kept pace, well back.

At the far end of the lake was a clubhouse Parker had never entered. The summer people used it for a number of things; then it was open weekends only, in fall and spring. It was closed now, the vehicles of a few maintenance workers clustered up against the low clapboard building. Parker turned in there, stopped among the other parked cars, and watched the black car, a Honda Accord with the mud of many miles on it, stream steadily by. The driver, alone in the car, was a woman. It was hard to see her face, because she was talking on a cell phone.

Parker pulled out of the lot and followed the Honda, pacing it the way she had paced him. She must have seen him back there but did nothing about it, kept a steady thirty-four miles an hour all the way around the lake, signaled for a right at the state highway, and turned north, toward the Mobil station.

And beyond. He followed her across the bridge at the Delaware Water Gap and into a mall on the other side. She drove to the parking area in front of a supermarket, left the car, went into the store. She was tall and slender, very blonde, in heels and jeans and black suede jacket over fluffy pink sweater. She looked urban, not rural.

Parker circled once, then took the nearest empty space, behind the Honda in the next row. He switched off the engine, sat there to wait, and a red Chevy Suburban pulled in next to him.

The gun Parker kept spring-clipped under the Lexus driver's seat was a small and lightweight .25 automatic, a Firearms International Beretta Jetfire — not much use beyond arm's reach but very handy in close. As a bulky guy got out of the Chevy on the far side from Parker and came around the front of his car, Parker reached under the seat, snapped the Beretta into his palm, and rested that hand in his lap.

The guy coming toward him wore black work pants, a dark blue dress shirt, an open maroon vinyl zippered jacket, and a self-satisfied smile. He had a big shaven head, a thick neck, small ears that curled in on themselves. He looked like a strikebreaker, everybody's muscle, but at the same time he was somehow more than that. Or different from that.

As Parker thumbed open his window, the guy came up to the car, leaned his forearms on the open windowsill, smiled in and said, 'How we doing today?' It was the gravel voice from the phone call.

Parker showed him the Beretta. 'One step back; I don't want blood on the car.'

The guy took the step back, but he also gave a surprised laugh and stuck his hands up in the referee's time-out signal, saying, 'Hold on, pal, it's too late for that.'

Too late? Parker rested the Beretta on the windowsill, his eyes on the other's eyes and hands, and waited.

The guy nodded toward the supermarket. 'Sandra's already been on the horn with the DMV. Claire Willis, East Shore Road, Colliver's Pond, New Jersey oh-eight-nine-eight-nine. Why don't you wanna have a nice little talk?'

'You're not law,' Parker said.

The guy shook his head. 'Never said I was.'

Being with a partner, running a license through Motor Vehicles, having all the time in the world for a stakeout, not particularly impressed by the sight of a handgun. 'You're a bounty hunter.'

'You got it in one, my friend,' the guy said, grinning, proud of either himself or Parker. 'If you're not gonna blow my head off, I can reach in my jacket pocket for my card case, give you my card.'

'Go ahead.'

'Not that a Beretta like that's gonna blow anybody's head off,' the guy said, reaching into his jacket, coming out with a card case. 'Though it would make a dent, I'll give you that.'

He extended a card, holding it flat between the first two fingers of his outstretched right hand. Parker put the Beretta hand in his lap again, held the card in his left, and read, *Roy Keenan Associates* and, under that, in smaller lettering, *Tracer of Lost Persons*. There was an 800 number, but no office address.

'Sandra's the 'Associates,'' Keenan said. 'What she walks around with mostly is an S and W three fifty-seven. I don't see her at the moment, but it could be she could see us.'

'You people like to talk.'

'Yes, we do,' Keenan said, with another comfortable smile. Then he said, 'Oh, I see, you mean she won't be quick enough on the trigger. You may be right, but what the hell, pal, here we both are. Why not let me say what I have to say, listen to what you have to say, if there's anything you want to talk about, and then you're done with me, and we don't have a lot of three fifty-seven Magnum bullets flying around a parking lot.'

'We'll talk in your car,' Parker decided.

That made him laugh again. 'Still worried about bloodstains, are you? Come along.'

12

The interior of the Chevy was laid out almost like a police car — a hunter's car, anyway. An over-under shotgun was attached by clips to the under part of the roof, and extra radios and scanners filled the space between the driveshaft hump and the bottom of the dashboard. The rear side windows were tinted glass with metal mesh inside, which would be for when a prisoner was in the backseat.

Keenan sat at the wheel, engine off and windows open, Parker to his right, hand in his pocket with the Beretta. Parker said, 'You want to talk.'

'Well, you know what I want to talk about,' Keenan said, 'I want to talk about Michael Maurice Harbin.'

'I didn't know those other names.'

'The impression I got,' Keenan said, 'that meeting you were all at, you were some kind of pickup group. Not long-term pals, I mean. A little more complicated for me, that's all. I'm not being nosy here, I don't wanna know what that meeting was all about, none of my business. My only business is Harbin.'

'I don't know where he is.'

73

'I believe that,' Keenan said. 'But I also believe one of the other fellas at that table just might know where he is. So the way it looks from here, if I'm going to find Michael Maurice, who has just absolutely vanished from the face of the Earth, I'm going to first have to find the rest of you guys from the meeting.'

'Starting with me?'

'Well, no.' Keenan gazed thoughtfully out the windshield. 'I started with Alfred Stratton. He was the one rented the room, and I noticed he used a false name and ID to do it, which slowed me down a little. But that was pretty interesting.'

'Maybe he doesn't want his wife to know he plays poker.'

'Maybe. He used a credit card in that phony name, though, that's pretty far to go for peace with the missus.'

'Not impossible,' Parker said.

'Well, let's just say that's something else outside my need to know,' Keenan said. 'I know there was a meeting. I know Stratton called it, and Harbin was there. Stratton has disappeared just about as completely as Harbin, so maybe they're both together, time will tell. But I got my hands on Stratton's phone bills, and the only thing interesting there was two calls to a guy named Nicholas

Dalesia, who it turns out has something of a record as a heister.'

'Is that so.'

'Not that I care. Anyway, I've been trying to make contact with this guy Dalesia, but so far no luck.'

'Another disappearance?'

'No, he's around, but he's in and out, he seems to be a very busy man, I just haven't managed to touch base with him yet. But I did get to his phone bill, and there's not much on it, but there's a call to somebody in New Jersey named Willis.' With a sidelong look at Parker, he said, 'You wouldn't be named Willis, would you?'

'Not usually,' Parker said.

'I thought not. Anyway, there's three other guys at that meeting I haven't tracked down yet, so it could be you could help me on that side. Or you might have some idea where I could find out a little more about our friend Harbin, who, after all, is the only and sole point of my entire inquiry.'

'Maybe he's dead,' Parker said.

'Show me where to dig.'

'Or maybe not.'

'Dead doesn't bother me,' Keenan said. 'If I can show proof of death, I collect just as much as if I walked in with the miscreant on the hoof. Mr Not-Willis, my usual livelihood comes from overly trusting bail bondsmen, but now and again some government reward money comes along that's rich enough to cause me to change my diet. I don't know what Harbin did or didn't do, but there's both state and federal paper out on him, and the combined jackpot is enough to get Keenan and Associates on the trail.'

'Then I'm sorry I'm wasting your time,' Parker said.

'Those other guys at the meeting.'

Parker shook his head. 'New to me. I believe they were new to Nick Dalesia, too, except for Stratton. Stratton called him and invited him. Then Nick called and invited me. He said I wouldn't know anybody else there, and he was right. Nothing came of the meeting, it turned out we weren't going to work anything out after all, so we went our separate ways.'

'I spend much of my life,' Keenan said, 'wishing I'd been the fly on this or that wall. Mr Not-Willis, far be it from me to cause you to leave bloodstains here and there around the world, but I want you to know, I am not going to be satisfied until I have my hands on either Michael Maurice Harbin or some certain sure proof of his death. I don't suppose you can help me find Nick Dalesia, either.'

'He travels around a lot, he's a busy man.'

'So I'm finding out.' Keenan shook his head. 'I know we'd both like it,' he said, 'if I could guarantee you we'd never see one another again, but I'm too much at sea here to say never again. You keep thinking about Michael Maurice, and any way at all that you could be of help to me, so that *if*, just if, I find I have to stop by and speak with you again, we don't have to spend a lot of time scaring each other with firearms.'

'Goodbye,' Parker said, and got out of the Chevy.

13

The problem was, what to do about Keenan? It would be best if nothing had to be done, at least not by Parker. If Keenan's search for Harbin would lead him sooner rather than later to McWhitney, the one who'd brought Harbin to the meeting, that would take care of it. McWhitney would at least keep Keenan busy for a while, and might even get rid of him. Somebody might eventually have to get rid of Keenan, one way or another. Having a bounty hunter rooting around in the background while they put together a bank job would not be a good thing.

What did Keenan know, and what didn't he know, and what did his knowledge mean? He knew there had been a meeting of seven men who weren't well known to one another. He knew Harbin was one of them, and he knew Harbin disappeared after that meeting. He knew there were rewards out for Harbin, sufficient to bring somebody like himself sniffing around.

But what didn't he know? The purpose of the meeting. The backgrounds of the people who were there. He had some low-level tipster somewhere in law enforcement, but he wasn't hooked in with the law in any major way. He could not have heard the tape, and so he probably didn't even know that Harbin had gone to the meeting wired.

All of which meant that Keenan wasn't getting much by way of help or input from the law. He was a freebooter, on his own, developing his sources and his information the hard, one-step-at-a-time way. If it became necessary to get rid of him, no lawman would care, or no more than usual.

As Parker had told Keenan, Dalesia was hard to get hold of. He had a phone but never answered it, had no machine on it, used it only for outgoing calls if he happened to be home. Parker could reach him eventually by sending a message to whoever was at that fax number Dalesia had given Elaine Langen. It would be good to let Dalesia know that this guy was lurking in the underbrush, but would it be necessary?

He hadn't decided that question when he'd finished the drive back from the conversation with Keenan, but then it turned out the decision had been made for him. He came into the house, found Claire in her swimsuit just coming in from the lake, and she said, 'Nick called. He left a number where you could call him, at six, or seven, or eight.'

It was now quarter past five. The number Dalesia had left would be a pay phone. 'I'll call him at six,' Parker said.

* * *

Outside the Mobil station where he'd waited in vain to see the Chevy Suburban was the phone-on-a-stick Parker used when he wanted to make a call that wouldn't be monitored for training purposes. He got there just at six with a pocketful of change and dialed the number in upstate New York, and Dalesia answered on the first ring: 'We got an event.'

'So have I,' Parker said. 'Would yours be the same one? A guy named Keenan?'

'No, mine is Jake Beckham. He was shot.'

'Shot?' That made no sense. 'The husband?'

'He's not that kind.'

'How bad is he?'

'Hit in the leg, above the knee.'

'In the hospital?'

'Yeah, for a couple weeks. Actually, it's not that far from where we wanted him, only now he's gonna have a limp.'

'This isn't what we wanted,' Parker said. 'We didn't want the law looking at him, wondering what he's been up to lately, what did he have on the fire, who's he been hanging around with.'

'That's true,' Dalesia said. 'We also didn't want Jake's reading on the thing.'

'Reading? What do you mean, reading?'

'Well,' Dalesia said, 'he thinks you did it.'

TWO

1

Gwen Reversa had decided to change her first name from Wendy even before she knew she was going to be a cop. The name Wendy just didn't lend itself to the kind of respect she felt she deserved. Wendys were thought of as blondes, i.e., airheads. Well, Gwen Reversa, now Detective Second Grade Gwen Reversa, Massachusetts CID, couldn't help it if she was a blonde, but she could help being a Wendy.

It was in a name-your-baby book that she learned that Wendy wasn't even a proper name all by itself, though that's what her mother had picked for her and that's what it said on the birth certificate. But Wendy was actually a *nickname*, for Gwendolyn.

Well. Once she'd discovered that, it was nothing at all to switch herself from a nickname without gravitas — Wendy — to a nickname with: Gwen. She was now twenty-eight, and at this stage in her life only her immediate family and a few early pals from grade school even remembered she'd once been a Wendy, and she was pretty sure they usually forgot.

'Detective Second Grade Gwen Reversa, CID,' she told the wounded man in the hospital bed, and he wheezed a little, nodded his head on the pillow, and said, 'Glad to see ya.' Would he be glad to see a Wendy? Nah.

'You feel strong enough to talk, Mr Beckham?'

'Sure, if I had anything to say,' he told her. 'They missed my lung by about three feet.'

She laughed, mostly to put him at his ease, and pulled over one of the room's two chrome-and-green-vinyl chairs. Since he was a crime victim, and the perp might be interested in a follow-up question, Mr Jake Beckham was in a private room.

Gwen took two notebooks and a pen from her shoulder bag, then put the bag on the floor and moved the chair so the shoulder bag strap looped around one leg, which is how you learned to keep control of your bag when you had a gun in it. Then she sat on the chair, opened one of the notebooks, and said, 'Want to tell me about it?'

'I don't know a hell of a lot about it,' he said. He was fiftyish, heavyset, weak and a little dour from having been shot, but there was nevertheless something boyish about him, as though, instead of lying around here in a hospital bed, he'd much rather be out playing with the guys. He said, 'I was just coming out of work — '

'Trails End Motor Inne.'

'Yeah, that's where I work, assistant manager. I was coming off my shift, I went out to my car — they want us to keep our cars out at the end of the parking lot — '

'Sure.'

'I was on my way, I felt this sting first, my right leg' — he rubbed it beneath the hospital sheet and blanket — 'I thought it was a bee sting, something like that, I thought, Jesus Christ, now I'm getting stung, and then, at the same time — See, I didn't hear the shot at first. I mean, I heard it, but I didn't pay any attention to it because I was distracted by this bee sting, whatever it was. Then I realized, my leg's going out from under me, that's something more powerful than a bee, and *then* I realized, holy shit, that was a shot! And there I am on my ass in the parking lot.'

'Did you hear a car drive away?'

'I didn't hear or see a goddam thing,' he assured her. 'I'm on my back on the blacktop, I'm suddenly weak, now I'm getting sudden-like light flashes around my eyes, I'm thinking, I was shot with a poisoned bullet! I gotta get outa here! That's what I'm thinking, and I try to roll over, and that's when I passed out, and woke up in the ambulance.'

'The bullet came from behind you.'

'Yeah, behind and to my right, cause that's where the bullet went in, halfway up between the knee and the top of the leg. They tell me the bullet's still in there, but it didn't hit any bone, they'll take it out in a couple days.'

There'd been very little to write so far in this first notebook. Gwen now opened the second, which contained the details she'd already collected, and said, 'So whadaya think? This the past catching up with you?'

He looked almost angry at that. 'Past? What past?'

'Well, Mr Beckham,' she said, tapping the notebook with her pen to let him know she had the goods, right in here, 'you have been known to hang out with the wrong kind of people.'

'Not any more!'

'You've done time — '

'All over!' He was agitated, determined to convince her. 'I did the minimum, got all my good behavior, that's *behind* me.'

'You're on parole right now.'

'Perfect record,' he insisted. 'You could check with Vivian Cabrera, she's my parole — '

'I've talked with her,' Gwen said. 'On the phone, before I came here.'

'Then she can tell you,' he said, pointing at the notebook as though wanting her to write all the good reports down in there. 'Not one black mark, no unacceptable associates, got a legitimate job, I learned my lesson, that's all over. And it was only the one mistake anyway. Over.'

'So,' she said, 'you have no idea who would take a shot at you.'

The way his face went, for just a second there, told a different story. His eyes shifted, his mouth skewed as though searching for some safe expression, and the whole countenance seemed to go slack with wariness, as though he'd just heard a dangerous noise. Then it was all swept off his face; he turned, round-eyed with innocence, and said, 'I been lying here, I been thinking about it, I mean, I got nothing else to think about, and I just don't get it. Maybe it was mistaken identity, because the guy was behind me, or just a wild shot, or I don't *know* what.'

He knows who did it, Gwen thought, or he thinks he does. The worst thing to do now, she knew, was confront him directly, push him, because then he'd just close up forever. She said, 'Well, we'll hope to find out from the shooter himself what he had in mind.'

'That's the way to go,' he agreed.

She tapped the notebook again. 'So who *do* you pal around with these days?'

'Oh, I don't know,' he said, and he was just a little too casual. 'There's some people at work I hang out with sometimes, that's about it. You know, the position I'm in, I gotta be very careful these days, I don't wanna mess things up after I built all this good record.'

'No, I can see that,' she said. 'You're smart to think that way. Any lady friends at the moment?'

'Nah.' He was being boyish again. 'You meet somebody, you know, you say you're on parole, it isn't a turn-on.'

Laughing, she said, 'For some women, it is. I've seen them.'

'Well, those are the ones,' he said, 'I shouldn't hang out with anyway.'

'You're right. Elaine Langen? See much of her any more?'

'Oh, my God, you even know about that! You sure checked me out, Det — What is it?'

'Reversa. Just Detective is fine.'

'OK. Anyway, you know everything about me, you know more'n I do, you don't need to ask me nothing.'

'Well, just in case,' she said. 'Elaine Langen, for instance.'

'That was a long time ago, Detective,' he said, and when he was being solemn like that, as though talking about a religious subject, he was more boyish than ever. 'That ended when I did the crime *and* I did the time.'

'You don't see her any more.'

'Not like *that*. We live, I don't know, seven, eight miles apart, I see her on the street, that's about it.'

'And her husband? Jack Langen, isn't it?'

'Yeah, Jack.' There was something dismissive in the way he said the name.

'Do you see much of him these days?'

'What, Jack Langen? I don't think I've seen him since I got out. Well, since I went in.'

'Do you think he holds a grudge?'

'Against me? After all this time? I — ' Then his face lit up with amusement. 'What, you think *he* did it? Shot me? Jack Langen? *He* isn't gonna shoot anybody.'

'You're sure of him,' Gwen said.

Beckham was sure. There was no faking now. He said, 'Jack Langen got even with me when he pressed charges and got me put away. The old man wanted to give me a pass. No, if anybody was gonna shoot anybody, and I'm not going to — No, I won't even say it.'

'But since you're not seeing her any more, there's no reason to.'

'Exactly.'

She tapped the notebook some more, looking at the history recorded there in her small, neat printing. There was too much emptiness in this life; there was something missing. She said, 'So you aren't close to anybody right now? You won't be having any visitors while you're in here?'

'Well, my sister,' he said, and suddenly lit up with triumphant amusement. Pointing at the notebook, he crowed, 'You didn't *know* about her!'

'That's true,' Gwen admitted. 'Tell me about your sister.'

'She's been living over in Buffalo,' he said. 'To tell you the truth, we haven't been so close for a while. Long time, really. But she got divorced last year, and one of her kids is in college and the other works for IBM, so when I called her to tell her about this she said she'd come help out while I'm laid up. You know, water the plants in my house and things like that. In fact, she's gonna stay in my house while I'm in here, she's driving over from Buffalo today, she might even be in the place by now. Well, not yet, she'll phone when she gets there.'

'Well, that's good,' Gwen said. 'You'll have family close by. What's your sister's name?'

'Wendy Rodgers.'

'So she's a Wendy,' Gwen said.

'Yeah. Wendy Rodgers. If she's keeping the husband's name.' Then he laughed and said, 'Well, she kept everything, the house, the kids.'

'I'm looking forward to meeting her,' Gwen said, and got to her feet. Picking up her shoulder bag, putting the notebooks and pen away, she said, 'If I think of anything else to talk about, I'll drop back.'

'Any time,' he said. 'I'll be here.'

She handed him her card. 'And if you think of anything that might be of some help to me, give me a call.'

'Will do.' He held the card as though it were precious.

'Bye for now,' she said, and as she waited for the elevator out in the hall, she thought, he lied twice, about not knowing who might have shot him and about his current relationship with Elaine Langen. But he doesn't think those two things are connected, he doesn't think the husband shot him.

There's somebody else in this story, she thought. Jake Beckham's life can't be that unpopulated. He's concealing something, and whatever it is, that's what shot him.

Maybe the sister, Wendy, knows. Be interesting to talk to her. But first, it would be very interesting to talk with Elaine Langen.

2

When the duty nurse told Dr Myron Madchen that a police detective was in with Jake Beckham, the doctor, in the first instant, thought everything must have come undone, that the detective must be here to arrest Jake and that everybody's plans were now destroyed, his not least of all, plus those of Jake himself and those two tough-looking fellows Jake had met with in his examining room. But then, on a moment's reflection, he realized that the detective must be here to investigate the shooting, that in this instance Jake was the victim, not the perpetrator.

'I'll wait till the detective's finished,' he told the duty nurse. 'Call me, I'll be in the staff lounge.'

She looked doubtful, but raised no objections. 'Certainly, Doctor.'

The fact was, as he knew full well, he had no real right to the staff lounge here, not being attached to this hospital or, at the moment, having a patient checked in here. Jake couldn't be considered his patient under these circumstances. Myron Madchen was Jake's primary care provider, but in this hospital it was the specialists who mattered, not the GPs.

Still, Jake was his patient in the normal course of events, and there was a certain professional courtesy to be expected in the circumstances, and no one would really expect him to go sit out in the regular waiting room with the civilians, so through the unmarked door he went and back to the area of peace and privilege of the staff lounge, a place rather like an airline's club members' lounge, but without the alcohol.

Sitting there, leafing through a recent *Newsweek*, he thought that in some ways what had happened was a positive thing. It was like the false hospitalization they'd been planning, but with the advantage that it was real; no lies had to be told.

Of course, the disadvantage was that a shooting would naturally draw the attention of the police. Would their presence interfere with the robbery? Dr Madchen sincerely hoped not. He sincerely needed that robbery. He sincerely needed it to save his life.

Some years ago, when Dr Madchen was at a very low point in his life, when he had reached a point where he wasn't sure he would be able to go on, he had happened to come across a very strange statistic in a professional journal. It seemed that a quarter century before, the state of California had done a statistical survey, using state records, to compare divorces and suicides according to occupation. One result showed that doctors of all kinds, except for psychiatrists, had the highest suicide rate and the lowest divorce rate of any occupation in California.

When Dr Madchen read that item, his immediate reaction was dread. He became as frightened as if a tiger had walked into his living room. He felt so threatened, so alone and vulnerable and helpless, that he had to stop reading and leave the house and go for one of the longest walks of his life, around and around and around his lovely, expensive neighborhood with its curving, quiet streets and broad green lawns and large, sprawling wood or brick houses, mostly prewar, set well back from the road.

It was late spring at that time, and the gardeners of the neighborhood had been hard at work, so the bright, hard colors of northern flowers were everywhere, backed by the eternal bass note of the dark pines. Dr Madchen, walking, looking at the beauty of his world, had thought, I don't want to die. I don't want to leave this. I have to remember that.

Because, in fact, suicide had been very much on his mind. On his mind but not acknowledged, the idea seeping into his brain like dampness in a basement until, without a drop of water having been seen to move, the entire basement is soaked.

He had been thinking about it, thinking about simply checking himself out of this life, thinking how easy it would be for him, as a doctor, to find a gentle, peaceful, painless way to end it all. That was what the article had suggested, that one reason doctors were so high on the suicide scale was because it was so easy for them and they could act with the assurance that they would neither hurt themselves nor make a mistake.

And the other reason, the article suggested, had to do with imagination. If a person in an unhappy life could imagine some other life, he was likelier to seek a divorce. If his training in the hard realities of medicine had left him unable to imagine another way out, he would reach for the sleeping pills. That was why writers and psychiatrists were at the extreme other end of the scale in that survey, having the highest divorce and lowest suicide rates. They were used to looking for new narratives, new connections. They could imagine a satisfying alternative to what they had, whether they ever achieved it or not.

I can imagine a different life, Dr Madchen told himself as he walked through that spring day. I can imagine . . . something.

But how? A loveless marriage was at the heart of Dr Madchen's unhappiness — a marriage entered into for cold reasons, a mistake from the beginning. He had married Ellen for her money, and it was still her money, and he was still tied to it. Ellen was a cold, vindictive woman, who begrudged him any thought that wasn't of her. To divorce her would be so grueling, so harsh, that of *course* he thought of suicide as the easier way. A divorce from Ellen — *that* he could imagine, and the image left him weak with misery.

Besides which, even if he managed to extricate himself from the marriage, what then? It was still her money. In fact, since she'd helped pay for his medical education and had entirely paid for his office, and given Ellen's disagreeability, she would no doubt not only keep all her own money but would also use her lawyers to beat some of *his* money out of him. No, no, it could not be contemplated.

One thing that article did do for him, however, was make him more self-aware and more open to anything at all that might bring comfort to his life. And his life needed comfort. He had come to believe, during that period, that many of his patients led much better lives than he did — even some with chronic medical problems, even those with quite serious illnesses. He could see happiness and hope in their faces, when he knew he had neither in his.

One of these patients was Jake Beckham, a hearty, rowdy man who would surely never put up with a woman like Ellen, not for (literally) a million dollars. Dr Madchen admired and envied Jake, and when Jake was arrested and imprisoned, neither the admiration nor the envy lessened. How staunchly Jake took his bad luck; how thoroughly he refused to be defeated. *There* was a man who could imagine another life for himself and make a leap for it, and so what if he failed this time? He would surely try again.

It was a happy coincidence that Jake wound up in the same state prison where Dr Madchen's worthless cousin, after years of drug addiction, had inevitably been placed. It had been to remain in contact with Jake as much as to be of help to Conrad that Dr Madchen had asked Jake to help the worthless man. And of course Jake had helped.

A very different kind of patient, toward whom Dr Madchen felt tenderness and pity, was Isabelle Moran, a healthy and beautiful young woman whose medical problems centered on an abusive husband. It was Dr Madchen who patched up the bruises and the sprains and the scrapes, while telling Isabelle time and again that she should report the husband to the police. But she wouldn't; she couldn't; she was too afraid.

When, shortly after reading the statistics article, he had to treat Isabelle once more, this time for a badly scraped knee, a broken rib, and a broken finger (the man always left her face alone), Dr Madchen realized that he and Isabelle were in one way very much the same: tied to a hateful spouse, unable to escape.

But they could console each other. They had been consoling each other for nearly three years now, secretly, hiding from the wrath of their spouses, and it had become, for both of them, intolerable. They had to get away, somehow. Neither could divorce, but both could flee. Or they could flee if they had money.

Jake, for Dr Madchen's assistance and silence and cover concerning the upcoming bank robbery, would give the doctor a third of his share of the take. A third.

He and Isabelle already knew they would go to California.

The wall phone in the lounge rang, and

another doctor, in green scrubs, went to answer it, then turned to say, 'Dr Madchen?'

'Yes,' the doctor said, dropping the unread magazine and getting to his feet.

'Your patient is ready.'

3

Feeling better about herself, feeling she had done everything she could to ensure her more pleasant future, Elaine Langen drove homeward in the crisp fall afternoon light and thought how she would miss the seasons here, if nothing else. Not this white Infiniti, beautiful as it was, and so much more like a glove she wore than a machine she drove. Not the house toward which she steered, full as it was of bitter memories. Not her past, her friends, her remaining relatives — all of them felt tired in her thoughts, a dusty and dogeared aura about them. Only the seasons — that's all that she would miss.

Not that the south of France doesn't have seasons — of course it does, but they're not the same ones. They don't contrast so much; they don't so often create their own excitement. Well, too bad. Once this bank business was over, Elaine was prepared to create her own excitement, on her own terms, in a setting of her own choice.

In the meantime, it was necessary to be amiable and accommodating with husband Jack just a little while longer. Jack was, she knew, her own damn fault, and the result of a rebellion against her father that had been wrongheaded to begin with. Harvey Lefcourt had been an authoritarian father, sure, but so what? He'd built Deer Hill Bank from scratch, and survived some very hairy economic times, too.

The fact was, when Harvey believed he knew what was best for his daughter, he was almost always right. Her angry feuds with him were not because he was wrong, but because he left her no space to come to the right answers on her own. Since he preempted the right, she had no choice, the way she saw it, but to defiantly claim the wrong as her own.

Thus, Jack Langen.

Well, it wouldn't be for too much longer, and in the meantime Jack wasn't particularly hard to get along with, all wrapped up as he was in the coming merger. A self-involved man, once he'd captured Elaine and the bank she sat on, he was content to let life just roll along.

Especially now, with this takeover that he'd insisted on, over her own objections and the posthumous objections of Harvey, relayed through Elaine. This was *not* a merger! It was a swallowing up, and Elaine knew it, and so did everybody else.

Well, Jack would be happy in the new headquarters of Rutherford Combined Savings, where he could play at being an old-money banker the rest of his life. And Elaine would be happy in the south of France, with all the money she'd need until she found the right well-off replacement for Jack. And Jake Beckham would be happy wherever he decided to go with his piece of the pie, so at the end of the day everybody's happy, so what's the problem?

Waiting, that's all.

But now, she arrived at the house, deep in the hilly countryside, rolling lawn and a three-story brick colonial with four white pillars across the front. Elaine had always thought the pillars a bit pretentious, but Jack had loved them, probably more than he'd ever loved Elaine, from the first time he'd gazed on them, bringing her home after their first date.

Elaine thumbed the garage opener on the visor, drove in, walked on into the house with one sack of groceries, and was barely in the kitchen when the front doorbell rang. She wasn't expecting anybody, so let Rosita get it; opening doors to salesmen was a job for the maid, not the mistress of the house.

'Mrs Langen.'

'Yes, Rosita?'

'Man here. Says you know him from the highway.'

'From the highway?' They weren't going to tear up the road again, were they? Let them not start until I'm safely in France, she thought, but said to Rosita, 'I'll take care of it,' and walked to the front door to see one of the bank robbers standing there. In her good cop, bad cop image of them, this was the bad cop, the one who never joked.

But good God, people like that weren't supposed to come *here*. Looking past him at the dark blue Lexus parked on the wide part of the drive, she said, 'What are you *doing*? We're not supposed to know each other.'

'I'm here for the gun,' he said.

At first she really didn't understand him. 'What gun?'

'The one you shot Beckham with,' he said. 'You want to talk about it out here, or in the house?'

'Shot — '

'Fine, I can talk out here.'

'No, no, come in. It's all right, Rosita!' she called, and led him down the hall, past the front parlor, to the smaller rear parlor, where they sometimes watched television. 'Sit down,' she said, 'and tell me what wild idea you seem to have.'

Since the chairs all faced the television set,

he half-turned one toward her before sitting down. Then he said, 'A pro would throw the gun away right after, but you're not a pro, and you are greedy, so you held on to it.'

'If you're saying I shot Jake — '

'We're past that,' he said. 'You did it, and sooner or later a cop is gonna show up here, and you've got a license for that gun. They'll want to see it. If you say you lost it, they'll get a warrant and search the house and find it and match it to the bullet they're gonna take out of Beckham.'

Being called greedy had overshadowed everything else he'd said. She said icily, 'I really don't see — '

'What happens to you, I don't care,' he said. 'But if they nail you as the shooter, the whole bank job comes undone. I don't want it undone.'

'Why on *Earth* would I try to kill Jake Beckham!'

'You didn't,' he said. 'You tried to put him in the hospital. When I told you, at that highway place, that he planned to miss a meeting with his parole officer, so he'd be safely in the can when the job went down, you said there was no need for that, nobody's gonna suspect Beckham anyway. But then, when he *didn't* miss the meeting, you realized, if he does draw attention to himself, he's also gonna draw attention to you. If he goes down, you go down. So you shot him, to put him on ice for a while, but you weren't smart enough to get rid of the gun, so — '

The doorbell sounded again, at the other end of the house. Irritated, she said, 'Now what?'

'Probably a cop.' He stood. 'Where's the gun?'

'I don't see — '

Rosita was in the doorway: 'Missus, a lady policeman here.'

Her heart leaped into her throat, and she stared at the robber, who didn't even seem to have heard what Rosita said. As quietly as before, he said, 'Where's the gun?'

'Kitchen,' she said, suddenly breathy. 'Top drawer, farthest right, near the door to the garage.'

He nodded, then said, 'The car out front belongs to a guy gonna do some landscaping. He's here to take measurements outside and then he's going, he's not coming into the house.' And he turned and left the room.

Elaine blinked at Rosita, then regained some control of herself. 'That man was not here.'

'No, missus.'

'I'll see the policeman in the front parlor.'

'Yes, missus.'

By the time she got to the front parlor, she was no longer visibly shaking, but she didn't look forward to being questioned by a policeman, not even a lady policeman. If that man had so immediately understood that she was the one who had shot Jake, and why, who else might see it? And he'd even known she'd keep the gun; he'd just assumed it, that she would be so careless.

She had to be careful. Starting now, she had to be very careful.

The lady policeman didn't look like a policeman at all, but was a very attractive blonde in her twenties, long-necked and slim-hipped, stylishly dressed in boots and slacks and a tan high-necked blouse. She was what Harvey would have called a thoroughbred. Why would such a person choose to be a policeman?

'I'm Mrs Langen. May I help you?'

'Detective Second Grade Gwen Reversa,' the woman said, and showed a gold badge in a dark leather case. 'I'm the investigating officer in the Jake Beckham shooting.'

'Oh, poor Jake,' Elaine said, praying she sounded innocent and shocked. 'You don't know yet who did it?'

'Not yet,' the detective said, and smiled. 'But there's always hope.'

'Yes, of course. Oh, I'm sorry, do sit down.

That's the most comfortable chair.'

'Thank you.'

They sat, Elaine on the sofa, the detective on the comfortable chair, and the detective first put her shoulder bag on her lap, then took a notebook and pen from it, saying, 'You've known Jake Beckham for some years, I believe.'

Elaine was astonished to feel a blush rising into her cheeks, but then was pleased by it, too; that would be a proof of innocence, wouldn't it, a blush? Cheeks hot, she said, 'Oh, Jake and I were a scandal, years ago. The one time I strayed from my marriage. I'm not proud of it, I can tell you that.'

'But you and Mr Beckham remained friends.'

'He's had so much trouble, poor man, and I suppose it's partly my fault. I take it you know about his imprisonment.'

'He stole from your husband's bank.'

'My father's bank. Well, it was then, but it's true, Jack, my husband, he was the one who insisted on pressing charges. Now I realize that meant he knew all about us.'

'You mean, if you hadn't been having an affair with Jake Beckham, he might not have gone to prison.'

'He definitely wouldn't have gone to prison. My father liked Jake, he would have been perfectly happy to give him another chance. But my husband was determined.'

The detective nodded, looking around the room, seeming to weigh it on some sort of scale. Then she said, 'Are there any guns in this house?'

'Yes, one,' Elaine said, and she couldn't believe what a close call that had been. 'I have a pistol,' she said. 'I even have a license for it.'

'But your husband has none?'

'No, Jack doesn't like guns. He says, 'I can argue, or I can run, but I don't know how to shoot.''

'But you know how to shoot.'

'Oh, yes. I took classes, I even used to go to the range and practice every once in a while. Haven't done that for years.' Smiling, trying for a lightness of tone, she said, 'I hope you don't think *I* could shoot anybody. Especially Jake.'

'Especially?'

'Well, he's a friend,' Elaine said, then leaned forward to emphasize the point. 'Nothing more than that, not since our *sordid* story all came out. But we've stayed friends. I had a drink with him, oh, two or three weeks ago. When I'm glum, you know, he cheers me up.'

'Yes, I can see where he would,' the detective said, and smiled again.

'Oh, you've talked to him, of course you have. How is he? I didn't think I should visit him in the hospital, I wouldn't want tongues wagging again.'

'He's in good spirits,' the detective said. 'Could I see this gun of yours?'

'Oh, I have no idea where it is,' Elaine said. Her heart was pounding, and for the first time she was uncertain she could carry this off.

The detective frowned. 'You don't know where it is? A gun is a serious thing, Mrs Langen.'

'Oh, I know, it's just — Years ago, I was taking women's defense classes and things, and the gun was just a part of all that, that empowerment everybody went through. After a while, I just lost interest.'

'Still, to not know where you keep a gun — '

'Well, I used to keep it in a kitchen drawer, near the door to the garage, so it would be handy if I were going to the range or whatever, but then Jack said, what if somebody breaks in, if they come in through the garage that drawer's the first thing they'll open.'

And it was true, Jack had said just that, several times, and she'd ignored him every time. She was used to ignoring things she didn't agree with.

'So then you moved it,' the detective said.

'I *think* I did. It could still be there, but I don't think so.'

'Could we take a look?'

'Miss — Ms — what do I call you?'

'Detective is fine.'

'All right. Detective, do you really think there's the slightest possibility *I* shot Jake? For what earthly reason?'

'Or your husband,' the detective said blandly. 'Or anyone else with access to that firearm. May we take a look, see if it's there?'

'Well, I suppose so,' Elaine said, and they both stood. As they walked together through the house, toward the kitchen, the detective said, 'Is that your Lexus parked out front?'

'No, that's a landscape man, he's here to do some measurements outside.' Again with a stab at girlish lightness, she said, '*He* wouldn't have access to the firearm, he's just measuring things outdoors.'

In the kitchen, she led the way to the right drawer and opened it, and there lay a small hammer, two screwdrivers, a small pair of pliers, three pencil stubs, and a box of cartridges for the gun, but no gun.

'You still have the ammunition, I see.'

'Yes.' Her hand shook slightly as she picked up the surprisingly heavy box. 'I don't know *how* old these are by now.' Opening the box, she said, 'About half left. It's really been a long time.'

Looking around, the detective said, 'Would you have moved it somewhere else in this room?'

'Or up to my bedroom, the closet there, I truly don't know. I'm really very sorry, but I'd stopped thinking about that gun ages ago.'

'It would be better if we could find it,' the detective said. 'I mean, just informally, without going through the process of getting a search warrant from a judge or anything like that.'

Feeling increasingly put-upon, Elaine said, 'Do we really have to make such a big deal over it?'

'If you'd like,' the detective said, 'I could phone for a few officers to just come out and look for it while we chat. They wouldn't disturb anything, I promise. Of course, if you'd rather check with your attorney . . . '

'No.' Elaine sighed, and that was as honest as the blush had been. 'Go ahead,' she said. 'Make your call.'

4

When Jack Langen saw the dark blue police van parked at his front door, next to a nondescript tan Plymouth Fury, his immediate thought was, What's she done *now*? He just took it for granted, if the police were here, it would be because of something Elaine had done. She was a prickly, difficult woman, and a part of the problem of her existence was the way she would suddenly spurt into action somewhere without the slightest thought for the consequences. So if the police were here, what had Elaine done now?

Thumbing the garage opener on the visor, putting his black Lincoln Navigator into the garage next to Elaine's white Infiniti, Jack told himself he shouldn't be hasty in his assumptions. Hasty, half-baked assumptions were Elaine's specialty, after all, not his. So if the police were here, and say for argument's sake it was *not* because Elaine had been stupid or careless, what reason might it be?

The bank move. The date for that had just been settled this afternoon. Elaine didn't even know it yet, unless the police had just told her. The four armored cars from Boston

114

would arrive here the night of October 4, just one week from today. Rooms for the four drivers and the eight accompanying guards had been taken at the Green Man Motel. The packing of over seventy-five years of correspondence and records and files and all the many kinds of necessary government forms had just begun. The cash reserves in the vault in the basement of the Deer Hill building would undergo a final audit in the two days before the move, being brought up to the bank itself starting after closing time on the fourth.

This was going to be the largest single act of Jack Langen's life. The company they'd hired to oversee the operation, Secure Removals, the American subsidiary of a British private security corporation, had already been on-site, and Bart Hosfeld, the manager in charge, had told him this afternoon that the closest thing in life to a move of this sort was an invasion in a war. 'Well, except,' Jack had said, 'there's no enemy shooting at you.'

'With this much money in cash floating around the midnight roads?' Bart had answered. 'Don't be that sure.'

A happy thought.

But that was why they were keeping the whole move as secret as possible, and why, he told himself as he got out of the Navigator and walked around the Infiniti and on into the house, it might very well be that the reason for the police presence at his house at this moment had something to do with the move.

But not. When he walked into the kitchen, a woman in police uniform was in there, wearing white rubber gloves and searching the kitchen drawers. She looked around when he entered, nodded and said, 'Good afternoon, sir.'

Nothing to do with the bank. Everything to do with Elaine. But why are they searching the kitchen? Jack said, 'Is my wife here?' half-expecting she was in a jail cell somewhere.

But the woman cop said, 'Oh, yes, sir, she's in the front room with Detective Reversa.'

'Detective Reversa.'

'Yes, sir. Excuse me, I'm almost done here.'

It was now twenty to five in the afternoon. Usually, when Jack got home from the office each day at around this time, he would make himself a small scotch and soda to begin the daily unwinding process, but he somehow couldn't see himself mixing a drink under the eyes of a uniformed woman cop searching for . . .

For what? What on Earth could this woman

policeman be looking for in Jack Langen's kitchen? What has Elaine done *now*?

Feeling stupidly awkward in his own home, Jack said, 'Well, um, nice to meet you,' and left the kitchen. As he walked through the house, bracing himself for whatever mess Elaine had made this time, he reminded himself that this difficult period of his life was very nearly over.

When he'd met Elaine shortly after college, with her family and her money — and her own bank! — the difficulties of having to deal with her seemed a small price to pay. Besides, old Harvey was still alive then, and could keep some sort of control over her.

Once the bank merger was complete, then he could make his move. Now, Elaine could still throw a monkey wrench into the process, but once the merger was a done deal, a very quiet little divorce would shortly ensue, and then Jack Langen would be a free and a happy man.

To have leveraged that chance meeting with Elaine into marriage and money and a career at the bank was wonderful enough for an impoverished nobody like Jack Langen, but now, to have leveraged her bank into a senior position of his own at a larger and more successful bank, run by a bunch of fellows with whom Jack could get along very well indeed, and in which Elaine herself was shuffled out of any position of power or importance, that was a coup of which Jack felt very justly proud. So all he had to do now was wait it out, wait it out, wait it out. No matter what Elaine had done this time, just wait it out. The end was in sight.

He couldn't *think* what this trouble might be. Not another affair; that business with Jake Beckham had been, Jack was sure, the most humiliating experience of Elaine's life. He knew that what she really wanted, and would always want, would be to get herself out of this corner of Massachusetts forever, go someplace entirely different, where no one would know what an ass she'd made of herself back home.

Well, after the divorce, she'd still be reasonably well off, so let her go where she wanted. Alaska, or some island.

Jack didn't realize he was smiling when he entered the front parlor, but then the smile faded, replaced by confusion when he saw Elaine sitting in there with a very good-looking young woman, a tall, svelte blonde of the sort Jack himself fancied from time to time, though never at home, never anywhere around here. *He* wouldn't make a public fool of himself, the way Elaine had, no matter what the woman looked like.

118

Though this one did look good. '*I'm* sorry,' he said to both of them. 'They said you were in here with a policeman.'

'I am,' Elaine said, and both women stood as Elaine said, 'This is Detective Reversa. Detective, this is my husband, Jack.'

Detective Reversa — who would have guessed? — put her bag back on her shoulder, as though she planned to leave, but then she smiled and stepped forward with her hand out, saying, 'How do you do, sir?'

'I don't quite know,' he said, receiving her firm handshake. 'I wonder what's happening here.'

'I'm the officer assigned to the Jake Beckham shooting,' Detective Reversa told him.

'Oh, *Jake*! That's right, he was shot, I barely registered that. We have a lot going on at the office right now.' Smiling, finding this whole thing amusing for some reason, he said, 'You don't think Elaine did that, surely. Rather late for a lovers' quarrel.'

'Jack,' Elaine said, in such a pained way that he looked more closely at her, and saw she was truly feeling miserable. He almost felt sorry for her. But then she said, 'They're looking for my gun.'

That made no sense. 'Your gun? It's in the drawer in the kitchen.'

'No, don't you remember?' she said. 'You told me I should move it because a burglar would find it right away.'

'And you moved it?' he asked, astonished that she would take his advice on any subject at all. 'Where to?'

'Well, I don't remember,' she said. 'That's why the police are here, looking.'

'It isn't a question of suspicion,' Detective Reversa assured him. 'It's just a loose end to be tied off, a gun owned by a friend of Mr Beckham.'

In other words, it damn well was a question of suspicion. Jack said, 'So I take it, there are policemen all over the house.'

'Not for much longer,' the detective said. 'Shall we sit? I understand your bank is about to make a major move.'

So we're going to chat, Jack thought, as all three sat. Looking at that pinched, nervous, unhappy expression on his wife's face, he was surprised to realize she hadn't lost the gun at all. She'd hidden it, or thrown it away.

For God's sake, why? Had she shot Jake Beckham? What for?

If our merry band of cops don't find that roscoe, Jack thought, and I'm pretty damn sure they're not going to, I am going to have to keep a very close eye on Missy Elaine until I've gotten her well out of this house.

5

It was all taking too long. Roy Keenan was not some soft salaryman somewhere, get paid every Friday whether he produces jackshit or not. A bounty hunter lived on bounties, and bounties were what you got when, and only when, you found and hog-tied and brought in your skip. The days and weeks you spent looking for your skip didn't earn a dime and if you never *did* find your quarry and lasso him home, you were just working for air all those days, brother, and let's hope it smelled sweet.

It didn't smell sweet, not to Roy Keenan. This Michael Maurice Harbin was turning out to be as hard to find as a deep-cover mole spy in the Cold War, which was ridiculous, because he wasn't any spy; he was a heister and a hijacker and a gunman. A lone wolf, like Roy Keenan himself. No connections, no goddam underground railway to keep you moving and out of sight. So why couldn't Roy Keenan, who could find the devil at a prayer meeting, come up with the son of a bitch?

The worst of it was, this time Keenan would be working for *less* than nothing if he came up empty-handed after all this. He had given a state cop in Cincinnati one hundred dollars for the information he had on Harbin and that famous meeting of seven men, which was the last time Harbin had been seen on this Earth. So he had *more* invested than just his own time here.

Sandra, Keenan's right hand, who would remain in a second car as backup tonight, a radio beside her that matched the one in Keenan's pocket, had come to the conclusion that Harbin was dead, and maybe she was right. Fine. Keenan didn't need the guy singing and dancing. A body was as collectible as a man, and easier to deal with. As he'd told that one wide boy, the one who wasn't really named Willis, if Harbin's dead, OK, just show me where to dig.

If he could figure out what those seven guys went to that meeting for, it might help. The few he knew anything at all about had records, and were all like Harbin: loner career criminals. But was it a heist they'd been planning? If so, they sure changed their minds. The seven had separated right after that meeting, about as far apart as if a hand grenade had been set off in their midst, and Keenan still hadn't found two of *them*.

Well, enough was enough. This time, he had a guy named Nelson McWhitney. He had him working as a bartender in a town called Bay Shore on Long Island, and living in rooms behind the bar. McWhitney had a nice, long record of arrests, and two falls. Apparently, he'd traveled to that meeting *with* Harbin, so why wouldn't he have traveled away from it with the same guy?

The nice thing about dealing with somebody who's already done two terms inside is that he's likely to be snakebit, to be wary and nervous and ready to give up most anything to avoid going back. So this time, Keenan decided, with this one he would press. He had too much invested in this fellow Harbin, time *and* money, and it was far too late to just let it go.

It sometimes helped if you seemed to already know all the answers to all the questions. It was bluffing, so it could be dangerous; it could backfire, but Keenan was desperate. He was ready to try anything.

And what he was going to try was the name Nick Dalesia. He had that name, and he had Alfred Stratton, and he had the guy who was or was not named Willis. He didn't know enough about Willis to use him as a source, and Stratton, as the organizer of that damn meeting, was just too obvious. The name Nick Dalesia should sound inside enough.

The bar in Bay Shore, deep and narrow,

dark wood, lit mostly by beer-sign neon, was probably lively enough on weekends, but at nine thirty-five on a Thursday night it was as dead as Sandra believed Harbin to be. Three loners sat at the bar, some distance from one another, nobody talking, and what must be McWhitney read a *TV Guide* as he leaned against the backbar. Red-bearded and red-faced, McWhitney looked like a bartender: a bulky, hard man with a soft middle.

Keenan took a position along the bar as separate from the other customers as possible, and McWhitney put his magazine open, facedown on the backbar before he came over to slide in front of Keenan a coaster advertising a German beer called DAB and say, 'Evening.' His eyes were surprisingly mild, but maybe that was because he was working.

'Evening,' Keenan agreed. 'I believe I'll have a draft.'

'Bud or Coors Light?'

'Bud.'

McWhitney went away to draw the beer, and Keenan thought how strange it was, even in a joint like this they offered you a light beer. The world was filling up with people, it seemed to him, who pulled their punches everywhere they went in life. Light beer, decaf coffee, low-sodium seltzer. About the only thing along that line that hadn't found a market was the grass cigarette.

McWhitney brought the Bud, and Keenan slid a ten onto the bar. McWhitney picked it up, tapped the bar with a knuckle, and went away to make change. When he brought it back, Keenan said, 'I'm lookin for a fella.'

McWhitney paused, hand above the dollar bills. The eyes got less mild, more concentrated. Moving his hand down to his side, he said, 'Yeah?'

'Mike Harbin. I was told you — '

McWhitney leaned back, holding on to the edge of the bar with one hand as he looked left and right at his other customers and called out, 'Anybody here know a Mike Harbin?'

The grunted nos that came back seemed to rise from people who were asleep. Before McWhitney could relay that response, Keenan grinned at him, pals together, and said, 'No, *you*, man. You're Nelson McWhitney, am I right?'

The eyes now were not mild at all. They peered at Keenan as though trying to read behind his eyes, into his brain. 'That's who I am,' he said.

'Well, then,' Keenan said, grinning as though there were no tension anywhere in the room, 'you're an old pal of Mike Harbin. I'm Roy Keenan, by the way. Nick Dalesia told me you know where I could find Mike.'

Puzzlement entered McWhitney's expression — puzzlement and something else Keenan couldn't quite read. 'Nick *Dalesia* told you that?'

A small voice inside told Keenan this might be a mistake he was making here, but he'd started now, so he kept on with it: 'Sure. I talked to him on the phone yesterday, at his place up in Massachusetts.'

'You've got Nick Dalesia's phone number.' Said flat.

'Right here in my pocket,' Keenan told him, patting the pocket. 'Why, you need to call him, check up on me?'

'I don't need to call Nick Dalesia,' McWhitney said. 'But he told you, did he, I know where Mike Harbin is?'

'Sure. He said you could help me. I mean, there's no trouble for anybody in this, I'm just looking him up for a friend.'

McWhitney leaned back again to look at his other customers, then came closer to say, 'I'll be closing pretty soon. Stick around, drink your beer, we'll talk after I close up.'

'Fine.'

Keenan sipped his beer and wondered if he should call Sandra to come in. To switch the radio in his pocket on and off would make one click on her radio, and she'd know from that to come in but not to know him, to be just another customer.

No, the problems with that were too many. A beautiful woman walking into this place at this moment would be just too strange. McWhitney would have to know that he and Sandra were connected somehow, and their pretending not to be connected would make him even more suspicious than he already was. And he wouldn't be able to shut the place if he suddenly had this new customer.

No, the thing to do was leave her out there for now, sip his beer, and wait for the other customers to realize it was time to go home.

Which took about fifteen minutes, during which time the drinkers at the bar peeled off one by one, calling, 'Night, Nels,' on the way out, and McWhitney responding to each by name. After the last one wandered out, McWhitney went around to lock the front door, and Keenan got off his bar stool to say, 'You know your customers.'

'I know most people who come in here.' Done with the door, he turned away and said, 'Come on in back, we can get more comfortable. Lemme show you the way.'

'Sure.'

McWhitney led the way to the end of the bar, where he paused to click off the lights behind them. Ahead were the restrooms and, on the left, a third unmarked door. McWhitney went to that one, pulled it open, and said, 'Shut it behind you, OK?'

'Sure.'

Keenan saw a small, cluttered living room as McWhitney switched on lights, then turned to shut the door. He turned back, and the baseball bat was just coming around in its swing, aimed at his head. He flinched more than ducked, so that instead of hitting his cheekbone and ear, the bat slammed into bone higher on the side of his head.

He staggered rightward, against the wall, throwing his arms up to protect himself, yelling, 'Wait! No! You got this wro — ' and the bat came around again, this time smashing into his upraised left arm, midway between elbow and armpit, snapping the bone there, so that the arm dropped, useless, and amazing pain shot through him.

McWhitney stood in a tree axer's stance, not a baseball stance. 'So Nick Dalesia's got a big mouth, does he? Thinks he's a comical fellow, does he?'

'No, no, not like that! Let me — '

'I'll see to Dalesia.'

This time the bat smashed his jaw and flung him again into the side wall. 'Naa!' he screamed. 'Naa!'

But the jaw wouldn't work. He'd always

used words; he was a talker; words got him into places and out of trouble, got him answers, got him everything he wanted; words had always saved him and protected him, but now all the words were gone, the jaw couldn't work, and all he could bleat was, 'Naa! Naa!' Even he didn't understand himself.

'Say hello to Mike Harbin,' McWhitney said, so at least he got the answer to that question, and the bat was the fastest thing in the world.

6

'I know, I know,' Wendy Beckham said into the phone, 'I was supposed to be here yesterday. Things came up.'

'That's OK,' her brother Jake said, from some hospital bed. 'I ain't going anywheres.'

Wendy pursued her own thought. A comfortably hefty woman in her mid-fifties, sensible from her neat gray hairdo to her flat shoes, Wendy Beckham Rodgers Beckham-again was used to pursuing her own thoughts, taking her own advice, making her own decisions, and helping out with the lives of those around her who needed help, whether they knew it or not. Like brother Jake, for instance.

'Family things,' she told him, 'got in the way. Family things always come up, irritating but they're your family, so you gotta do it. You wouldn't know about things like that.'

'Come on, Wendy, not while I'm down.'

'You don't sound down.'

'Then bring my tap shoes, we'll go dancin'.'

She took a deep breath. As usual, she had to fight aggravation just thinking about her baby brother, who would never stop being her brother, but would also never stop being a baby. 'You're right,' she said. 'I'm busting your chops, and I shouldn't do that.'

'Not till I'm on my feet.'

'I'll just write everything down,' she said, 'so I can wham you with it all at once, when you're feeling better.'

'Then I'll feel even better. When you coming over?'

'When are your visiting hours?'

'Eight a.m. to six p.m.'

'All day?'

'Well, I'm in a private room here. Wait'll you see it. Better'n my house.'

'Jake, if you can afford that,' she said, judgmental and suspicious and not caring if she was, 'I don't wanna know *how* you can afford it.'

'Hey, listen, I got shot,' he told her. '*I* don't pay for all this. I'm a crime victim over here.'

'There's a new role to play. Listen, I gotta unpack, buy a couple groceries — you don't stock up much around here — '

'Yeah, yeah.'

'OK, I'm not busting your chops. I'll get there around two, OK?'

'Unless family things come up.'

'Now who's busting whose chops?' she

said, and hung up, and turned to the job of unpacking.

She'd never been in Jake's mobile home before, but wasn't surprised by what it looked like: a neat, compact, old-fashioned design with an overlay of Jake-the-slob. There were more dishes in the sink than on the shelf, and it had been a *long* time since anyone had cleaned the toilet or mopped the floor. Catch *me* being your housemaid, she silently announced, but she knew, before she got out of here, she would have done a lot of tidying up. And the worst of it was, Jake wouldn't even notice.

Fortunately, he didn't have that much clothing, so she could shove it all out of the way and put her own garments on hangers and shelves. His bathroom gear was at the hospital, leaving plenty of room — filthy sink — for hers.

She was just finishing up when a knock sounded, weirdly, on the metal door. Mistrustful, expecting no one, Wendy inched to the door, leaned against it, and called, 'Who's there?'

'Police.' But it was a woman's voice.

Police? Something to do with the crime victim, no doubt. Wendy opened the door, and this didn't look like any cop to *her*. A blonde stunner, tall and built, in a peach satin blouse under a brown leather car coat and black slacks. But she did hold up her shield for identification as she said, 'Wendy Beckham?'

'That's me.'

The cop smiled as though she knew a good joke about something, and said, 'I'm Detective Second Grade Gwen Reversa, I'm assigned to your brother's shooting. May I come in?'

'Sure. I just got here,' Wendy explained as the detective entered and Wendy shut the door. 'Sit down anywhere. I'm still unpacking.'

'I asked the beat cop to keep an eye on the place,' Detective Reversa said, 'let me know when you showed up.'

They both sat in Jake's sloppy yet comfortable living room, and Wendy said, 'I was supposed to get here yesterday, but there's always last-minute fires to put out on the home front. I just called Jake at the hospital, he certainly sounds OK.'

'It's not a bad wound,' the detective told her. 'The bullet's still in there, in the flesh, but it didn't hurt anything serious. They're supposed to take it out tomorrow. I'm looking forward to getting it to the lab.'

'I bet you are. You got any suspects?'

'As a matter of fact, yes, two of them,' the

detective said, with another pleased smile. 'But before I say anything about *my* idea, let me hear yours. Do you have any suspects?'

'Me, no.' Wendy hesitated, but the detective's silence encouraged her to go on. 'I don't know how much you know about my brother.'

'Military police, bank security, stole from his employer, went to jail, got out, on parole, works for a motel not far from here. No more black marks on his record.'

Laughing, Wendy said, 'I'd say, you know him about as well as I do. The thing is, since Jake and I both grew up, I'm talking about thirty years now, we haven't exactly lived in each other's pocket. Our parents are dead, neither of us lives in the old neighborhood. When I have family get-togethers these days, it's *my* family, my kids and my in-laws. I got a divorce a while ago, but it was a strange kind of settlement. I got the kids, the house, the car, and his parents, who can't stand him. He got the bank account, but that's OK, I get it back in alimony and child support.'

'He's good about that.'

'He's one day late, his parents are all over him. He's a lawyer, he makes good money, he doesn't want that trouble, and also he can afford it. Can you imagine you're talking with an important client, your secretary says your mother's on the phone, you have to say 'No! Tell her I'm out!'?'

The detective laughed, and then said, 'The point is, Jake really isn't very much in your life, or you in his.'

'Almost nothing, until this getting-shot business. It happened I had time on my hands. I was probably feeling a little guilty anyway, so I said I'd come here, help out while he was laid up. But who his friends are, who his enemies are, all of that, I haven't known that kind of thing about him since we were both in high school. And he didn't much want me knowing even then.'

'Sibling rivalry.'

Wendy shrugged. 'He was a shortcutter, and I wasn't. So who are your suspects?'

Again the detective laughed. 'You know,' she said, 'you just don't seem too much like a Wendy to me.'

'I don't?' Wendy didn't get it. 'Why? What's a Wendy supposed to be like?'

'Not so forceful.' Smiling, the detective said, 'You ought to become a Gwen, like me. They're both from the same name, you know. Gwendolyn.'

'I didn't know that,' Wendy said. 'What is it, you don't want to tell me about your suspects?'

Another laugh: 'There, you see? Forceful.

No, I'm happy to tell you, because so far, they're only suspects. Before your brother went to jail, he was having an affair with the wife of the owner of the bank.'

Wendy said, 'What? His employer? He's dipping *and* he's dipping?'

'It all came out when they caught his embezzlements,' the detective said. 'Everybody insists it's all over, and maybe it is, but when I went to see Mrs Langen yesterday — '

'The wife.'

'The wife. She has a pistol permit, and is registered with a Colt Cobra thirty-eight-caliber revolver. It's a very light, small defense gun, it weighs less than a pound, she probably carries it in her purse, when she carries it.'

'Doesn't sound much like a banker's wife.'

'Some women got into that women's self-defense idea some years ago. That's when she got the gun. The trouble is, yesterday, when I asked to see it, she said she'd lost it.'

'Sure she did,' Wendy said.

'Up to that point,' the detective said, 'I really wasn't considering her at all. If there are guns in the story, you want to see them, have they been fired recently, is the serial number one that will show up here or there. So when she said it was lost . . . '

'Oh ho, you thought,' Wendy said. 'It's her.'

'Well, there's also the husband,' the

detective said, 'which is why I said I had two suspects. Either of them could have taken the gun and shot it at your brother. If the husband did it, and then threw the gun away, then the wife is telling the truth. As far as she knows, it's lost.'

Wendy said, 'So what are you gonna do?'

'Wait for the bullet to come out of his leg, first thing tomorrow morning. If it's a thirty-eight caliber, we'll bear down.' Looking around the room, she said, 'I know you want to unpack and get over to see Jake. Tell him I'll drop in on him tomorrow afternoon, when we know about the bullet.'

'I will. But first, shop.'

★   ★   ★

When she came back from the supermarket, Wendy found herself envying those residents of Riviera Park who had those rusty little red wagons chained behind the office, for carrying their groceries home. As it was, she had two plastic sacks of necessities, and nothing to do but lug them on down Cannes Way and around the corner onto Nice Lane, where a tall man in a dark gray suit stood outside Jake's pea-green mobile home.

She kept on, though she didn't like the look of him, but then saw a big candy box in his hand and thought, Oh, it's a getwell present for Jake. How unexpected.

Yes. 'This is for Jake,' he said when she reached him, and lifted off the top of the candy box, and inside was a gun.

'Oh!' Startled, she jumped back, the grocery sacks dragging her down; she expected him to take the gun out of there and shoot.

But he didn't reach into the box. Instead, he said, 'Tell him, this is the one did it.'

Wide-eyed, she stared at the gun again. 'Shot Jake? This is the gun?'

'Somebody told me Jake thinks I'm the one put the plug into him,' the man said. 'Tell him, if I had a reason for him to be dead, he'd be dead.'

Now that the gun wasn't being used to threaten her, she leaned closer to it, studying it. It was black. The handle was crosshatched, with a white circle at the upper end that showed a rearing horse under the word COLT. The same design, without the circle, was cut into the black metal of the gun above the crosshatching and below the hammer. The cylinder was the notched fat part, where the bullets would be and would revolve one step every time the gun was fired. The barrel was a stubby thing, with a simple sight on top and the word COBRA etched into the side.

'Oohh,' she breathed, 'It's *hers*.'

'You know about her.'

'The police said.' Still wide-eyed, she gazed at the man's cold face. 'She's a suspect.'

'She didn't do it to put him down,' the man said, 'but to get him out of the way for a while. You tell him when you go see him.'

'I will.'

He closed the box and tucked it between her left side and left arm. 'You keep this,' he said.

'I will.'

And later, at the hospital, in the very clean private room, she said, 'Jake, you have some bad companions.'

7

'He makes a perfect ex-husband,' Grace said.

Monica, who had one husband, no exes, shook her head yet again, and said, yet again, 'Well, to me it seems weird.'

The two women, who clerked together in the claims office of one of the big insurance companies in Hartford, and who had been pals since both had hired on here almost ten years ago, were similar in kind: both rangy and sharp-featured, both pessimistic about life in general and their own lives in particular, and both choosing to face the world with a kind of humorous fatalism. They disagreed about very few things, but one of those things was Grace's ex, a subject that tended to come up, as it had today, while they were on their ten a.m. coffee break in the ladies' lounge, where they could have some privacy.

Monica was going to do the litany again, no stopping her. 'You never see him,' she said.

'A good thing in an ex,' Grace said. 'I got a memory bank full of pictures, I ever want to go stroll down there.'

'But I mean you *never* see him,' Monica

insisted. 'I don't think anybody ever sees him.'

'No, that's pretty true,' Grace admitted. 'I guess he's like the tooth fairy in that.'

'The *tooth* fairy!'

'Or Santa Claus. You know he's been, because the tooth is gone or the presents are there, but you never see him at work.'

'Grace, he's a criminal!'

'Another good reason not to see him at work. If people see Nick at work, they'll dial nine-one-one. Right away.'

'Let me say this about Harold,' Monica said, referring to her husband, which sooner or later she always did. 'Harold may not be the most exciting man in the world, or the most brilliant man in the world, but at least he's *there*. And when he puts bread on the table, he puts it there with the sweat of his brow.'

'With the ink of his brow, you mean,' Grace said. 'Monica, he's an *accountant*.'

'You know what I mean. It's honest money, honestly earned, and it puts honest bread on the table. Grace, you're living off a gangster!'

'He is not,' Grace said. 'In the first place, he's not a gangster, he's a heister, which is a very different thing. Gangsters deal in prostitution and gambling and drugs, and Nick would never do any of that. In his own way, he's almost as law-abiding and moral as your Harold.'

'That's why he's in hiding all the time?'

'He's not in *hiding*, he's just very careful, because you never know. The world he's in is full of dangerous people, so he's smart to be cautious.'

'Harold can walk the street in the sunshine with his head up high and not be afraid of anything.'

'Monica, Harold lives in the world of accountancy.'

'Don't try to make Harold sound dull.'

'That wasn't my intent.'

'Anyway,' Monica said, 'not that I ever expect anything like this for myself, God forbid, but you don't even have proper alimony.'

'That's the other thing I was gonna say,' Grace told her. 'I'm not living on Nick, I get a salary here, same as you do. I get a supplement from Nick.'

'When he feels like it.'

'Which is often. From time to time I can help him out a little, pass a message on, whatever, and from time to time he helps me out a little, with a money order. It probably works out to more than alimony anyway, and there's no lawyers involved, no judges, no bad feelings on any side. Honest to God, Monica,

I understand why you think what you think, but I'm telling you, I've got the best ex-husband in the world, because I never have to confront him, I never have to argue with him, and I never have to be mad at him.' With a little grin, she added, 'And in addition, I've got Eugene.'

'Oh, Eugene,' Monica said, with her own little grin, because both women agreed that Eugene was a total stud muffin. Unfortunately married, but nobody's perfect.

'Never you mind Eugene,' Grace told her, though she had no fear that Monica might poach. 'You just go on feeling sorry for me over Nick.'

'I don't feel *sorry* for you,' Monica insisted. 'I just think it's weird, that's all. Well, you heard me on this before. Time's up, anyway.'

Back at her desk, Grace saw that a fax had come in. It was just the one sheet of paper, blank except for a large, scraggly handwritten 4.

This was precisely the sort of thing Monica would find weird, so Grace had never gone into detail with her about the kinds of favors she sometimes did for Nick. He'd phoned her about this a few days ago, that a fax would come in containing a number from one to thirty. He didn't tell her what it was about, and she didn't want to know.

So here it was, and now she was to phone Nick. He wouldn't answer — he didn't even have the ringer on at his place, wherever that was — but after ten rings a light would go on, and she'd hang up. On her way home today, she would stop at the public library and go to the hardcover mystery section, and put the folded fax into *The Gracie Allen Murder Case*, by S. S. Van Dine, which was always there, and then she'd continue on home.

And in a little while, a nice money order would arrive in the mail. What was so weird about that?

8

The bullet coming out was worse than the bullet going in. Not the instant of it — they had him doped for that — but the aftermath. The anesthetic wore off slowly, leaving him dazed, with a jumble of dreams he couldn't remember, couldn't even understand when they were going on, except that some of them seemed to have something to do with prison. Happy goddam thing to dream about.

What brought him out of the daze finally was the discomfort. They had his leg in a sling hung down from a contraption over the bed, so it was up in the air with the heel pointed at where the ceiling met the wall to the right of the room door. He was like that, and would be for the next few days, because they didn't want him to lie on the wound for a while. But that meant he couldn't move much of himself at all, except his arms.

His leg hurt like hell, once he was conscious again. It felt much worse than when he was shot, like a really hard punch that just wouldn't ease up.

There was a television set on a shelf high on the wall, and he tried watching it for a while, but everything he saw irritated him. So after a while he switched the thing off and just lay there, alone with his thoughts.

Alone. They'd told him, no visitors right after the operation; he'd be too woozy. But he wasn't woozy exactly; he was just uncomfortable, with the leg aching as if a dinosaur had just bit him there, and stuck up at an angle so he couldn't get comfortable even without the ache.

He spent a lot of the time thinking about yesterday's visit from Wendy. The amusing part was her meeting with Parker. It took a lot to knock Wendy off her pins, but Parker had done it. Jake wished he could have been there when Parker opened the candy box and showed her the gun. She was still a little green around the gills when she'd told him about it.

The other things she'd told him were more serious, and they all had to do with the fact that it was *Elaine* who had shot him, and she'd shot him so he'd be in the hospital at the time of the robbery and wouldn't be a suspect. Stupid Elaine; where did she ever get that bright idea?

If he'd known she was going to react this way, the hell with it, he'd have skipped his parole officer meeting after all; he'd have gone to Vegas or someplace and checked himself into a county jug.

But the worst thing Wendy'd told him was that the woman detective, Reversa, *thought* maybe it was Elaine that had done it. Elaine or the useless husband — she was ready to go either way — but the problem was, she was already pointed in the right direction.

She didn't have any motive yet, not for Elaine, but thought maybe she had one for the husband. But when the robbery went down? Here she had a woman linked both to the bank and to the guy that was shot, her onetime and maybe still boyfriend. Here she had a woman whose gun was conveniently lost just at the right moment. Here she had a robbery of that bank just when all its assets were being transferred. And to put the cherry on the icing, the mysteriously shot guy was an ex-con with former associates of the wrong kind, what Wendy yesterday had called his 'bad companions.'

Was that enough for Reversa? Would she look at what she had, and connect the dots? Jake might not remember those anesthesia-induced prison dreams, but he remembered prison, and he didn't want to go there again.

Maybe the job was no good. Maybe Elaine had screwed it up for everybody, and now it was nothing but trouble.

And if it *was* trouble, some of the other

people might take it on the lam, but Jake himself wouldn't get far, on his back in a hospital bed with his leg pointed at the ceiling.

Come to think of it, the trouble was probably exclusively for Jake and Elaine. Parker and Dalesia could go ahead as planned. So far as they were concerned, nothing had changed.

Jake was beginning to feel desperate. This was some miserable bind he was in, all of a sudden.

What if . . . what if he could give Detective Reversa a different motive, one that didn't have anything to do with the bank? But what motive would that be? 'Oh, yeah, Detective, I think you're right, Elaine shot me, because uhh . . . '

And then what? Yeah, we're seeing each other again? How does that get me away from the robbery? If Elaine is the one that shot me, then that ties me to the robbery.

But what if it was Jack? Oh, he's wrong about us, we aren't seeing each other any more. But if he's wrong, and there's no evidence, why would he suddenly turn into this violent guy he'd never been before?

It made Jake's head ache, along with all the other parts that already ached and itched and burned. It made him so frustrated, this unexpected problem looming down on him, that he did get woozy, and dropped off to sleep, and when he woke up, Detective Second Grade Gwen Reversa was sitting there in the chair beside the bed.

'Oh, good, you're awake,' she said with a bright smile.

'I'm not supposed to have visitors,' was the first thing he thought to say, because he wasn't ready to deal with all this, to deal with Elaine and this keen-eyed cop and the fact that Parker and Dalesia had nothing to worry about. *They* had nothing to worry about.

'Oh, I get special dispensation,' Detective Reversa told him, still with that sunny smile he didn't trust for a second. 'I promised I wouldn't stay long, and I wouldn't get you all upset.'

'Well, good luck with that,' he said.

She cocked her head, smiling and alert. 'Really? Why do you say that?'

'Because if you're here,' he said, scrambling to keep his mind ahead of his mouth, and also feeling ridiculous because he was lying here in front of this fine-looking woman with his leg aimed upward like an antiaircraft gun, 'if you're here, that means you think you know more about who shot me, and anything you want to tell me about that is going to upset me.'

'Well, there is news, you're right,' she said. 'We now know more about the bullet that was used.'

'Well, sure,' he said. 'It isn't in me any more, so you could look at it.'

'It was a thirty-eight Special,' she said. 'Do you know anybody with a gun that uses that ammunition?'

'I don't know anybody with a gun at all,' he said. 'When I was in security, and before that in the police, I was around guns, but not any more.'

'It's hard for me to remember,' she said, 'you used to be on the police yourself.'

'Not like you,' he said. 'Not a detective. I was just the guy who waved at the traffic.'

'But the fact is,' she said, 'you do know at least one person who owns a gun.'

He frowned. 'I do?'

'Your friend Elaine Langen.'

'Oh, my God!' he said. 'She told me that years ago!' I hope I'm not overdoing this, he thought, and then, trying to tiptoe his way through the right reactions, he frowned at her and said, 'You don't think *she* did it.'

'Not necessarily,' she said. 'We do know it was the right caliber. Unfortunately, Mrs Langen has lost her gun.'

'Lost? How do you *lose* a gun?'

Detective Reversa's smile turned ironic.

'That's a very good question, Mr Beckham,' she said. 'But really there's another question first.'

'There is?'

'Well, two people had access to that gun,' she reminded him. 'Both Elaine Langen and her husband.'

'Oh, because it's in the house.'

'Exactly.' Leaning forward, being concerned, being *on his side*, she said, 'If it turned out that Mrs Langen's gun *was* the one that shot you, which of the Langens would you guess might have used it?'

This was the nub, the hinge. This was the point where, if he was ever going to get out from under what Elaine had done to both of them, he would do it now. He would find the words. He would deflect the investigation, take it off somewhere far from the robbery.

She watched him, smiling faintly, in no hurry, and he thought, I can't put it on Jack Langen. I would love to, but no way. 'No way Jack Langen would shoot me,' he said.

She looked surprised. 'You seem very positive of that.'

'In the first place,' Jake told her, 'he's got no reason to be sore at me, not any more, not for years. And in the second place, that isn't what he'd do, it isn't the way he operates. If Jack Langen wanted me shot, he'd get somebody else to do it. And he wouldn't loan the guy his wife's gun.'

'No, I don't suppose he would. So you think Elaine did it.'

He turned away from those sharp eyes, that fake smile. Elaine did it; yes, of course, Elaine did it. They were going to know that, if they didn't already. They might not ever be able to prove it, but they'd know it. 'I'd hate to think so,' he said.

'Because you were very good friends.'

Well, he didn't have to put up with that much irony. Facing the detective again, he said, 'I had an affair with Elaine Langen. It was never going anywhere, we were never gonna run away together, and we both knew it. Then her husband must've found out the same time he found out I was stealing. He got his revenge, he pressed charges, he paid me back, it's all over as far as he's concerned.'

'*Is* it all over? Between you and Mrs Langen, I mean.'

'Absolutely,' he said, and all at once he saw it. The road out of the woods. 'She wanted to start up again,' he explained, 'when I got out, but I'm done with *all* of that, every bit of it. I'm Mr Straight-and-narrow. I told her, it can't pick up like before, it just can't.' Then he allowed himself to get a bit wide-eyed. 'Holy shit.'

Alert, she said, 'Yes?'

'You're right. She did it.' Hushed, he said, 'Elaine took a shot at me.'

'That's what you think happened.'

'But, listen,' he said. 'Think about it. Look where she shot me,' and he pointed up at his inclined leg.

'Yes?'

'She's a good shot, Elaine,' he said. 'She told me, she used to go to the firing range and practice all the time. So if she did shoot at me, and OK, maybe she did, but if she did, she wasn't trying to kill me.'

Detective Reversa looked skeptical. 'Why would she do that, Mr Beckham?'

'She was trying to attract my attention,' Jake said. 'She really can't stand her husband, I can tell you that, but she's stuck with him, and for a while there I helped her sort of put up with the life she had to lead. I went into prison, I came out, I said no, she got desperate — I don't mean I'm some kind of fantastic lover or anything, I'm just the guy that made it easier for her to live her life, that's all. I was like, I don't know, like her Valium. And I said no. And she brooded about it, and she decided, let's attract his attention.'

Looking and sounding honestly amused at the idea, the detective said, 'And to let you know, next time it could be worse.'

'That's it,' he said. 'Jesus, Detective Reversa, I bet you that's just what happened.'

'You could very well be right.'

'And she threw the gun away. At least she threw the gun away. Though she could buy another. Or maybe she just hid it. But I don't care, I don't want to press charges.'

'She *shot* you, Mr Beckham.'

'I understand that,' Jake said. 'But I understand why she did it, and I understand it was a felony for her to do it, and if you can catch her on your own, that's fine. But I don't want to help. I'm sorry I said as much as I did.'

Detective Reversa considered the situation, then nodded. 'For your sake, Mr Beckham,' she said, 'I hope Mrs Langen appreciates your gesture.'

9

Nelson McWhitney was a bartender to begin with, but the bar he bought from his former boss never did make much of a living. A few of the regulars in the place, though, were connected to another line of work that was certainly more profitable but also chancier. Still, when these guys began to invite Nels along, he was happy to go. At first, he was just brought in for the heavy lifting, or the muscle if muscle were needed, but after a while he got to know some things, like how to open certain safes, how to bypass certain alarm systems, and his value to his partners only increased.

Unfortunately, mistakes by a couple of those partners had led to two brief stints inside, where he'd picked up a wider acquaintance, so he could pick his future partners with better care.

One of the first things he'd learned, way back, was never to trust those partners for a second. A thief is a thief. If he's stealing anyway, he might as well steal from his partners, if he gets the chance.

It had been a long while since Nels had

given anybody that kind of chance. With his mistrust of his partners had come a certain pragmatic wariness and a habit of protecting himself in certain ways. For instance, if he was going to be working with this fellow or that fellow, he liked to know where the fellow could be found later on, just in case.

Whatever the dental gold job with Al Stratton might have turned out to be, it had aborted before Nels could do that kind of homework on the rest of the group, including Nick Dalesia, but Al Stratton he could find, and Stratton would know how to put Nels together with Dalesia.

He hadn't expected such stupidity from Dalesia. A man had died at that meeting. You don't make jokes about it. You don't hint to strangers — and a bounty hunter, no less! — that Nels McWhitney could tell you where to find Mike Harbin. That's just stupid.

What was it for? Revenge maybe, because Nels had brought Harbin to the meeting? Whatever Dalesia's reason, it was stupid, and Nels was looking forward to asking the question in person.

Which meant going to visit Al Stratton, who in his straight life was a furniture refinisher in a small town outside Binghamton, New York. Stratton had taken what had originally been a dairy farm, sold off the grazing land, lived in the farmhouse, and converted one of the barns to a workplace where he had room enough for any piece of furniture a customer might want dealt with.

Like most people who live some distance from town, Stratton kept a couple of dogs on the place that would let you live once their master said you were OK. McWhitney drove in from the county road, and as he circled the old wood-shingled house, both dogs came tearing out of the barn, yelping and throwing themselves around, snapping at the moving tires as McWhitney crunched along the gravel to stop at the barn's open door.

He kept the car windows closed, and one of the dogs lifted his forepaws onto the driver's door, onto the ledge just under the window, and dared McWhitney with a snarl. The other dog, still on the ground, ranged back and forth, barking.

Until Stratton came out and yelled at them. Then they immediately turned away from McWhitney and went trotting over to Stratton, who came a pace closer to peer through the windshield. When he recognized McWhitney, he nodded, waved, and said something more to the dogs as he pointed at the barn. Obediently they went inside, not bothering to look back, and Stratton came over to the side of the car as McWhitney rolled his window down.

Stratton said, 'You surprised me.'

'I don't like to talk on the phone.'

'No, I understand that.'

Stratton could be seen trying to figure this out. He and McWhitney didn't hang out together, had only a work relationship and not much of that.

'I need to find Nick Dalesia,' McWhitney explained. 'I figured you know where he is.'

'Well, I *did*,' Stratton said. His eyes were watchful.

'The thing is,' McWhitney said, 'there's a fella has maybe a job, and if he does have it there's maybe a spot in it for me. But he doesn't know me, and he does know Nick, though not where he is. But I need Nick to tell this guy I'm OK, and also maybe see if he wants a piece in it.'

Stratton nodded. 'Any more pieces around?'

'It's not my pie, Al. Sorry.'

'I understand. I think I got a phone number for Nick.'

'The way I've been told, Nick never answers his phone.'

'I think he lives over in Connecticut or Massachusetts,' Stratton said. 'I may have an address. You wanna come inside?'

'I don't know,' McWhitney said. 'Do I?'

Stratton grinned. 'Oh, don't worry about

the dogs. Once I tell them you're all right, you're all right. Unless you start beating on me.'

'I'll remember not to,' McWhitney said, and got out of the car.

He followed Stratton into the barn, which looked mostly like a stage set for some upscale family drama. It was all clean, but not particularly neat. A couple of old-fashioned sofas stood around among armoires, dining tables and chairs, some smaller tables, and a dry sink. Some of the items looked very good; others were in several pieces. Toward the rear of the place, the dogs were lying on old, scuffed blankets. They watched McWhitney, but didn't move.

Stratton led the way to an old rolltop desk against a side wall. 'Customer never paid me for this,' he said as he rolled the top up out of the way and sat down. 'So it's mine now.'

'It's a beauty.'

The desk's pigeonholes were full of notepads of various sizes, thick envelopes, some folders. Stratton reached into the jumble, pulled out a smallish address book with a dark red cover, and said, 'I only do first names in here, so that's how they're alphabetized. Here we are. Nick.' Pointing to a corner of the desk, he said, 'Take a scrap of paper there, and a pencil.'

'Sure.'

'Box twenty-three, County Route forty, Greengough, Massachusetts.' Stratton spelled the name of the town. 'Box numbers are hard to find sometimes.'

'Oh, I'll find it,' McWhitney said, pocketing the address. 'I'm motivated.'

10

Nick Dalesia drove the roads between Deer Hill and Rutherford, with side trips to and past West Ruudskill, where they would take the armored car. Because the countryside was hilly and had been settled for a long time, there were multiple routes between any two points. Some roads dead-ended where an early settlement hadn't lasted, leaving nothing but a family name: Granthornville. Some roads went out of their way to loop past a water source that hadn't been needed in two hundred years. It was terrain a heister could make good use of, but first he'd have to learn it.

The way Dalesia figured it, the people doing the move would not be the regular bankers but professionals, hired because this kind of move is what they do. They would try to keep the move secret, but they would know that leaks are just part of the human condition, and that at least some unauthorized people out there would know, by the time of the move, that the move was going to happen. Among those unauthorized people there might be some who would fantasize about getting their hands on all that money and all those securities, but would there be a few who might decide to take an actual run at it? Such robberies had happened before.

Yes, they had, and Nick knew they had, just as much as the bankers did. It had happened in America, it had happened in France, and it had happened in Germany that he knew about, and probably other places, too. And the MO was always the same: A gang, ten or twenty strong, would lie in wait along the route, pop out, kill or otherwise get rid of the drivers and guards, and drive away to some field or parking lot where the getaway cars were stashed. The fast ones didn't get nabbed while making the transfer; the slow ones did.

The job Dalesia and Parker were putting together was different. No gang, only the two of them. And they only needed to pluck out one armored car from a caravan of four.

So it was very important to find the right place to do it. They needed an intersection, small and tight, that they could dam with the disabled armored cars they'd leave behind. They needed that intersection to give them a good, easy run toward the abandoned mill in West Ruudskill where they'd make the switch, without it being obvious from where they pulled the job exactly where they had to be going.

So Dalesia these days was putting a lot of mileage on the car. His job was the terrain, Parker's the materiel. They would need guns, and they would need other things as well. Parker was off promoting the gear they wanted, while Dalesia traveled the county roads, looking for just the right intersection.

And he believed he'd found it. It was not part of any town, but it had a little commercial buildup around it; a café open only for breakfast and lunch, a gas station that shut at dark, a used-car lot with cars behind a chain-link fence and with a small shed out front with a handwritten sign on the door: PHONE FOR APPT.

The area was occupied, but not at night. The roads heading north and east met other turnoff roads almost immediately, making an escaper's route very hard to guess. At the intersection itself, the two roads coming up from the south and east met at dogleg angles, no straight lines. And the diner, the used-car shack, and the layout of the gas station made for a somewhat constricted area around the intersection. The armored cars would have to come through very slowly.

For breakfast and lunch, the diner's parking lot at the front and left side was full of pickup trucks. This was where the labor force in this part of the world ate everything

163

but dinner. They were all regulars, talking to one another about their jobs and their bosses and their favorite sports teams. They paid no attention to Dalesia when he sat among them and spent some time over coffee at a window table at the front, looking out at the intersection, pleased with his choice.

The point was to be here before the armored cars arrived, to set themselves in useful positions. They had a rough idea how to pull it off, and how to lead the target car away, but where should they place themselves to begin with? The armored cars would come up that road over there, to cross the intersection northbound. Parker and Dalesia would want their special one to go out the road on that side, they would want the other three armored cars to block the intersection there and there, and the more Dalesia looked at the place, the more it seemed to him they needed two guys on the ground and one to bird-dog the target.

Three. They needed one more man.

Dalesia paid his check and left the place, thinking about people he knew, wondering if Parker might know somebody who'd be available almost any minute now. He walked around the side of the diner, and at first he didn't recognize the guy seated on the passenger side in his car, just thought,

164

somebody's in my car. Why?

Then he saw it was McWhitney, one of the guys from Al Stratton's meeting, the one who'd carried Harbin away, and he grinned as he walked over and opened the driver's door to say, 'You're just the guy I'm looking for.'

McWhitney showed him the automatic in his right hand and said, 'I don't think I am, Nick. Get in.'

Something's wrong, Dalesia thought, and he thought, something's wrong with *me*. I didn't expect him, I didn't know why he was all of a sudden in my car, and I just walked up to him grinning like an idiot, as though nobody'd ever been dangerous to anybody in the whole history of the world.

I'm still alive, anyway, Dalesia thought, as he got behind the wheel. Maybe this is only bad, not worse than bad.

Since he had the stupid smile on his face anyway, he left it there and said, 'What's wrong? Nelson, isn't it?' I don't even know this guy, he told himself, and I walked right up to him. I deserve whatever I get.

McWhitney said, 'I just have one question, Nick.'

'Sure. Go ahead.'

'Why'd you wise off?'

'I'm sorry?' Thinking, this son of a bitch is

gonna kill me for a mistake, an error, he said, 'Wise off to who? About what?'

'Oh, you been talking to a lot of people?'

'I haven't been talking to anybody,' Dalesia said. 'Except Parker. You don't mean Parker.'

McWhitney looked uncertain, and then certain again. 'I don't give a shit about you and Parker,' he said. 'I mean you and Roy Keenan.'

'Never heard of him,' Dalesia said, because he never had.

Now McWhitney was angry. 'Never heard of him? You talked to the guy about Mike Harbin and you never *heard* of him?'

'Oh, for Christ's sake,' Dalesia said, 'you mean the bounty hunter.'

'Oh, you do know him.'

'No, and I don't want to. Parker told me about him. He found Parker, but Parker brushed him off. He says the guy doesn't know anything, he doesn't even think he ever heard the tape Harbin made.'

McWhitney frowned mightily. 'Keenan never talked to you.'

'Never.'

'He did talk to Parker.'

'He's looking for all of us,' Dalesia said. 'He's looking for you, too, because there's some kind of reward money on Harbin. But he doesn't know anything.'

'He found me,' McWhitney said.

Dalesia looked at the automatic, now resting in McWhitney's lap. 'Is that why the hardnose?'

McWhitney sighed and slipped the automatic out of sight under his jacket. 'I'll tell you what happened,' he said. 'I fell for an old one.'

'Yeah?'

'This guy Keenan, he comes to me, he says you told him he should ask me where to find Harbin.'

Dalesia laughed. 'Why would I do that?'

'That was my question. What were you up to. But it wasn't you up to something, it was Keenan. That's the old dodge, he tells me you told him this thing or that thing, then I'm supposed to figure it's OK to tell him more.'

'He had no idea what was going on.'

'None,' McWhitney agreed.

'So that was a big mistake he made.'

'Yeah, it was.'

Dalesia grinned. 'I bet he learned a lesson from it.'

'Yeah.' McWhitney nodded. 'He learned the harp.'

THREE

1

'I like retirement,' Briggs said. 'Turns out, I was nervous all those years.'

'You looked nervous,' Parker said.

And it was true; Briggs looked calmer than the last time Parker had seen him, after a broken heist where Dalesia had been the driver, Parker and Tom Hurley and a guy called Michaelson had been the doers, and Briggs the explosives man, fussy and petulant but very methodical behind his thick spectacles. When an alarm had gone off that hadn't been in the plan they'd been sold, Michaelson wound up dead, Hurley went off for revenge, but the guy who'd sold them the plan had disappeared forever, and Briggs decided he'd had enough. 'I'm running a streak,' he'd said. 'A very bad streak. I believe I'll just retire for a while, and wait for it to go away.'

He'd already had this house in Florida, not on either coast but inland, on a lake near Winter Garden. He had a wife, too, but she wouldn't be coming out to see their visitor, and Parker wouldn't be going inside the house. He and Briggs sat on a patio in front of one corner of the low, broad house, facing the lake glittering like a diamond pin out there, where motor-boats snarled and white sailboats slid silently among them at a slant.

Watching the movement on the lake, Parker said, 'You like things calm. No commotion.'

'We get commotion sometimes,' Briggs said. He'd put on a few pounds but was still basically a thin unathletic man who looked as though he belonged behind a desk. Nodding at the lake, he said, 'A few years ago, a tornado came across from the Gulf, bounced down onto the lake, looked as though it was coming straight here, lifted up just before it hit the shore, we watched the tail twist as it went right over the house, watched it out that picture window there. That was enough commotion for a while.'

Parker said, 'You watched it out a picture window?'

Briggs either shrugged or shivered; it was hard to tell which. 'Afterwards, we said to each other, that was really stupid.'

'So you want to stay retired,' Parker said.

'The last time we met,' Briggs said, 'we were crawling through a tunnel with alarms going off. Michaelson got shot. I don't want any more of that.'

'Let me tell you what I've got,' Parker said.

'I don't need you there, when it goes down. I need materiel.'

Briggs looked doubtful. 'You want me to sell stuff to you?'

'I want you to provide it,' Parker told him, 'for a piece of the pie. Come along and show how it works, but then be somewhere else when it's going down.'

'What materiel do you need?'

'I need to stop three armored cars, and open one more.'

'That's a lot of armored cars.'

Parker told him the setup, and Briggs said, 'Using them as roadblocks, that's nice.'

'You're the one knows what would work.'

'Well, a lot of things would work,' Briggs said. 'I'll tell you something I can get my hands on. You know the Carl-Gustaf?'

'Sounds like a king.'

'It's an anti-tank gun, made by the Swedes, ever since the Second World War. It's heavy, but you won't be carrying it except in cars.'

'How heavy?'

'Thirty-six pounds, a little over four feet long. It's eighty-four millimeter, shoots different kinds of rounds, including anti-tank. The anti-tank shell is almost six pounds all by itself.'

'It sounds old,' Parker said.

'But it's still in use,' Briggs assured him.

'The NATO countries used it a lot. Singapore's got two hundred of them right now, Uganda uses them. There's a place in India makes the ammunition.'

Parker said, 'And you can get hold of some of these Carl Gustafs.'

Grinning, Briggs said, 'I'm retired, but not that much. The difficult part, these days, you start dealing in arms, the feds figure you're probably hooked up with terrorists. Makes it hard for a private guy to get along. But the good thing is, I know people who have materiel they're afraid to move, because anybody they talk to could turn out to be undercover. And one of these people I know has Carl-Gustafs.'

'Could you get them to New England by October fourth?'

Briggs considered. 'Five days from now? I'll drive them up in my van.'

'Good. One of the people with us manages a motel, we can put you there without paper, so you never left home.'

Briggs nodded, smiling at his lake. 'That's the goal, all right,' he said. 'Never leave home. What else do you need?'

'To get into the last armored car without setting fire to anything.'

'They'll have a radio in there,' Briggs pointed out. 'And a global positioning device.'

'I know that,' Parker said. 'So it all has to be fast.'

'You'll want an Uzi or a Valmet or something like that, to shoot out the tires and the door locks. Do you worry about the guards?'

'If they're sensible,' Parker said, 'it's better to leave them alive. Doesn't get the law as agitated.'

'I agree. So the three Carl-Gustafs and two assault rifles. Do you want tear gas?'

'Then we'd need masks,' Parker said, 'so we could go into the car to get the goods, and everything slows down. No, it's up to the guards. They get out of the way or they don't.'

'I suppose so.' Briggs frowned out at the lake. The noise of the motorboats, an irritation at first, after a while seemed to become a part of the day, like the droning of insects. Briggs said, 'In my years on the heist, I never liked it when somebody died. I still think about Michaelson from time to time.'

'That wasn't us,' Parker said. 'He was shot by a guard.'

'He was dead.'

Parker said, 'I don't want these armored car people dead, but I'm not going to have a lot of time to spend on them.'

'No, that's true.'

'We're giving them the choice, that's all.'

Briggs looked troubled, but then he said, 'Let me tell you something I learned about retirement, I mean, besides it's boring.'

'Yeah?'

'It's expensive. Where in New England am I meeting you?'

2

Dalesia picked Parker up at Bradley International Airport in his Audi, and they drove north toward Massachusetts. Along the way, Parker said, 'Briggs is aboard. He's got stuff we can use, he'll drive it up, but he doesn't want to be in on the job.'

'I was thinking, though,' Dalesia said, 'we could use a third man.'

'You say that,' Parker said, 'as though you've got him.'

'Well, don't you think we do?'

'I've been thinking the same thing,' Parker said. 'Who've you got?'

'McWhitney.'

'McWhitney? Where did he come from? The last time I saw him, he was carrying Harbin out on his back.'

'Remember the bounty hunter braced you a little while ago?'

'Keenan or something.'

'He made a mistake with McWhitney,' Dalesia said. 'He came on like one of the guys, but he didn't know anything about anything, so when he told McWhitney *I'd* said he should ask him how to find Harbin,

177

McWhitney didn't like it.'

'No, he wouldn't.'

'He let Keenan know, and then he came looking for me.'

Parker looked at Dalesia's deadpan profile. 'He believed Keenan?'

'He did for a while.' Dalesia grinned, as though there'd never been a real problem. 'We worked it out,' he said, 'and I asked him aboard. It seemed to follow. If you don't like the idea, I think we'll have to sneak up behind him. He's a jumpy kind of guy.'

'No, McWhitney seemed all right,' Parker said. 'We gotta talk a little, though.'

'Yeah, he'll meet us there.'

'There?'

'Turns out,' Dalesia said, 'this is a good time to slip some extra guests into that motel where Jake works, without bothering the official records.'

'I told Briggs we'd put him up there, while the job was going down.'

'We're all there,' Dalesia said, 'you and me and McWhitney. Seems right now there's an annual slump in their business there.'

'Oh, yeah?'

'The truckers they got all the time, but the civilians taper off around now. The people that did their summer vacation in Maine, the people bringing their kids back to college, that's all done. Now there's nothing till next week, when they have what they call the leaf peepers, the people that come out from the cities to watch the leaves turn red. We're outa here before they show up.'

'Good.'

'I've been doing some other stuff, too,' Dalesia said. 'I found the intersection where we do it, it's perfect for us, I'll show it to you this afternoon. That and the church.'

'The church?'

Dalesia was enjoying his surprise. 'Wait for it. We'll have some lunch with McWhitney, and then I'll show you around.'

'You've been busy,' Parker said.

'Well, we've only got four days.'

★ ★ ★

Since they weren't actually registered at Jake Beckham's place, Trails End Motor Inne, they didn't have lunch there but at a 'family' restaurant nearby. McWhitney drove his own car to meet them there, arriving second, and when the hostess walked him toward their table, Parker said, 'He looks irritable.'

'He doesn't know if you're gonna love him.'

Neither did Parker. He hadn't picked up much of a sense of the man in that first meeting that Stratton had set up; only McWhitney's wide-eyed dumb show of innocence when it had turned out that Harbin was wired, and the immediacy of his silent acknowledgment that it was his responsibility to make Harbin disappear. Which he had done, well enough to confound even a professional bounty hunter.

But was this irritable look also an irritable nature, and would it matter? Dalesia had described him as a 'little jumpy,' and Parker could well believe it. But, if his jumpiness wouldn't get in the way, it would be a good thing to have a third in the string, particularly when there were armored car guards to handle, and later, when the faster they switched the cash to their own vehicle the better. And Parker could see where, at a moment when McWhitney had been not only jumpy, but suspicious that Dalesia had ratted him out, it had seemed to Dalesia a good idea to offer him a job.

McWhitney stopped at the table to shake both their hands, he standing, they seated. He didn't bother to smile during the handshake, but said to Parker, 'Good to see you again.'

'You too.'

'Maybe this time it'll come to something,' McWhitney said, and sat down.

'It's coming to something, Nels,' Dalesia

said. 'Parker's got the hardware on the way.'

McWhitney nodded. 'Good.'

They were interrupted by the waitress. The menu was printed on the paper place mats. They ordered things, and then McWhitney said, 'I understand you met that guy Keenan.'

'Yes.'

'I take it he didn't push you very hard.'

'Not hard,' Parker agreed. 'He didn't know anything, so he didn't know where to reach for a handle.'

'Well, he made a grab at a handle when he came to me.'

Dalesia said, 'Sounds as though he was desperate by then. Time going by, not getting anywhere, no profit in sight.'

McWhitney nodded. 'I think he was in the wrong business,' he said.

Dalesia grinned. 'Well, at the end he was.'

Their food came, and while they were eating it, McWhitney said to Parker, 'Did Nick talk to you about some church somewhere?'

'He said the word 'church,'' Parker said, 'but he didn't say what it meant.'

'Same with me,' McWhitney said. He turned his dissatisfied gaze toward Dalesia. 'Look at him,' he said. 'He looks exactly like somebody with a concealed full house.'

Dalesia was pleased with himself. 'That's just what I am,' he said.

They all traveled in Dalesia's car, McWhitney in the backseat. Dalesia showed them the intersection first, where they would grab the armored car, and they both approved the choice. McWhitney, gesturing at the diner and the gas station, said, 'These places are empty at night?'

'Nobody out here at all.'

Parker said, 'I like the way it narrows down.'

'Let me show you where we go from here,' Dalesia said. 'The car we want we'll take out this way, to the right.' He drove less than half a mile, then stopped where a dirt road angled off to the left. 'We stop the car here,' he said, 'put the guards over on the dirt road there.'

Parker looked around. The area was hilly, the road twisty, with pine woods along the right and on part of the left. Just beyond the dirt road turnoff, a cornfield had finished its season and was turning into papyrus. 'Not much traffic.'

'Don't open a lemonade stand,' Dalesia advised, and drove them on.

West Ruudskill was seven miles farther. They didn't stop, but Dalesia told McWhitney, 'That's our mill, where we'll switch the cash from their armored car to our truck. Big wide doorway, solid floor.'

'Looks good,' McWhitney said, peering out the back window at it as they drove by. Facing front again, he said, 'I guess, next it's this church of yours.'

'Eleven miles from here,' Dalesia said. 'All crap road, twisty, two-lane, but at least it's all paved.'

They drove to the end of the road from West Ruudskill, and Dalesia took the left where it came to the T, then in a quarter mile another right; and a few miles later, after passing a few farms but mostly woods, he turned off on the right side at a small white clapboard church with a wooden steeple. Across the road was a narrow two-story white clapboard house with a broad porch around the lower floor. Both buildings had the look of long disuse.

'These country churches,' Dalesia said, pulling in at a weedy gravel area that would once have been a parking lot, 'they're losing their congregations, doubling up, nobody can afford to keep every one of these dinky things going any more.'

They got out of the car, and Dalesia said, 'The power's off, here and across the street. The line still comes in, so maybe we could start the electric if we needed to.'

'We shouldn't need to,' Parker said.

'That's what I figure.' Dalesia started off around the church, saying, 'Let me show you what I like about this place.'

Around back, a large white-clapboard-sided lean-to had been attached to the rear of the church some time after the original construction. The slanted roof was gray asphalt tile, and the addition was completely open across the back, almost the full width of the church. The covered space was about ten feet from front to back. A few miscellaneous items were jumbled into a rear corner, but the rest of the dirt-floored space was clear.

'There's bits of their old Christmas manger scene back there,' Dalesia said, pointing at the stuff in the corner. 'They built this on for storage, I guess back when congregations were getting bigger instead of smaller. But you know what's great about this?'

'The truck,' Parker said.

McWhitney smiled for the first time since Parker had met him. 'We put it in sideways,' he said. 'We cover it with a tarp, so there's nothing shiny.'

'Run your helicopters,' Dalesia said. 'Do what you want. We're inside, safe and dry, and our stash, in the truck, is out here, invisible.' He grinned around at them, proud of his discovery. 'Myself,' he said, 'I've always been a churchgoer.'

3

Back at the family place for breakfast next morning, Dalesia was irritated. 'I went home last night,' he said, 'check on things. My signal was on that wasn't supposed to be on. The person we had the missus send the fax to.'

Parker said, 'She sent another fax.'

'To my intermediary contact,' Dalesia said, 'who didn't like that. And neither do I. I told the missus, at the beginning, lose that number.'

'They never do,' Parker said.

McWhitney paused with a lot of pancake halfway to his mouth to say, 'You always have to go back and take it away from them.'

'That's what we're gonna do,' Dalesia said. He sounded grim.

Parker said, 'She wants another meet.'

'Noon today, same place. Just one of us, she says.'

'Me,' Parker said.

Dalesia frowned at him. 'Why you? It's my message system.'

'She's got you upset. I can stay calm and still get the number out of her.'

Dalesia wasn't sure he liked that. 'Or?'

Parker shrugged. 'Or it turns out, she was afraid the cops were getting too close, coming in on her for shooting Jake, she didn't see how she could go on.'

McWhitney said, doubtful, 'She offs herself?'

'Only if she's that stupid,' Parker said.

'With me she'd be that stupid,' Dalesia said. 'OK, Parker, you do it. Nels and me, we'll get some bottled water, candy, shit like that, stash it in the church.'

⋆ ⋆ ⋆

At noon, Parker stood by his Lexus in the rest area parking lot as before, and here came the white Infiniti down the lane. He held up a hand to stop her, walked around the hood, and slid in on the passenger side.

Frowning at him, she said, 'Aren't we going in the restaurant?'

'You don't want coffee. You bring that fax number with you?'

'Of course not, why would I do that?'

'Because my partner told you to get rid of it and you didn't. So now you will. No copies, nothing.'

'I don't see why it's such a big deal,' she said. She hadn't started driving yet, since

Parker had climbed in.

'You don't have to see,' he told her, and nodded at the windshield. 'Drive on, don't be conspicuous.'

'This isn't the way it was supposed to be,' she said, but she put the Infiniti in gear and drove it through the parking area, a moving advertisement for milk.

'We can do it one of two ways,' Parker told her. 'We can drive to your place, you go in and get the number, and any copies you made, and bring it out and give it to me. Or you can take me back to my car and I'll go to your house myself and search a little.'

'Oh, my God, no.' The threat seemed to raise a host of horrible visions in her mind. 'All right,' she said. 'We'll go there, I'll get the number.'

'Along the way,' he said, 'you can tell me what this meeting's about.'

She frowned, not speaking, and steered them out of the rest area and eastward on the MassPike. Up to eighty, along with everybody else, she said, 'The policewoman knows I did it.'

'You're out walking around,' he said.

'She can't *prove* I did it, but she *knows* I did it. She doesn't know why. Jake's tried to convince her it was because he wouldn't come back to me, and that I wasn't really trying to kill him, I was just trying to make him pay attention to me, but she isn't sure she buys it. She isn't dumb.'

'That's too bad,' Parker said.

Elaine Langen gave him a quick sidelong glance. 'Because I am?' When he didn't answer, she said, 'As soon as there's a robbery, she'll know Jake was lying, she'll know we're both involved.'

'As you say,' Parker said, 'she can't prove it.'

'Maybe she can.' Elaine Langen was very upset. 'She'll *know* it, and she'll poke and pry, she'll look for inconsistencies, she'll question me and question me, and I don't know if — '

'Don't say that,' Parker said.

She looked at him, not understanding. 'Don't say what?'

'Don't say you'll cave in and tell this woman everything you know,' Parker told her. 'Don't say that to me, don't say it to my partner, don't even say it to Jake.'

'But I don't — '

'Whichever one of us you say it to,' Parker interrupted, 'will kill you.'

She swerved, the car jolting as she stared at him.

'Stay in your lane. You don't want to attract a trooper.'

'No, I — ' She controlled the car, but not herself. Leaning forward over the wheel, staring wide-eyed and open-mouthed out the windshield, as though seeing some horror on the far horizon, she said, 'How can you say that? How can you just say a thing like that?'

'Because it doesn't have to happen. I'm giving you advice, Mrs Langen. You're in something very deep. It's over your head out here. You gotta keep swimming. If you don't keep swimming, you're gonna drown. No use blaming me for it, or my partner, or Jake. You swim, or you drown.'

'You drown me.'

'Easily. You're dead before you can worry about it.'

They had reached the exit. She steered the Infiniti down the ramp, and Parker pointed at a diner some distance away. 'Pull into the parking lot there.'

'I'm afraid to stop.'

'I don't have that fax number yet. Pull in.'

She pulled in, switching off the engine, and sat with both hands on the steering wheel, eyes fixed on the dashboard. 'What now?'

'You were going to say,' Parker told her, 'call it off, the cops are too close, they're suspicious already, we can't go through with it.'

Blazing up, forgetting to be terrified, she

turned her head to glare at him, fingers clutching the wheel even tighter as she said, 'That's right! And it's true, they *are*. They're suspicious, they believe I shot Jake, they don't really buy the reason Jake gave them, if this robbery happens they'll know that's the reason. They'll just come after me. I don't know how strong I am.'

Parker said, 'Remember you decided, my partner and me, we're good cop, bad cop?'

She didn't follow. 'Yes?'

'This woman cop you've got.'

'Detective Second Grade Gwen Reversa.'

'Is she good cop or bad cop?'

'Good, at least so far. I mean, she's on her own. So there is no bad cop.'

'Yes, there is,' Parker said. 'Me.'

The look she gave him turned bleak.

Parker said, 'Everything she says to you, every hour she spends on you, just keep reminding yourself. This is the good cop. The bad cop is out there, and he's not very far away, and he doesn't go for second chances.'

'I'm sure you don't.' Her voice now was a whisper, as though all strength had been drained from her.

'The bad cop is nearby.'

She closed her eyes and nodded.

'Talk to the good cop all you want,' Parker said. 'But always think about the bad cop.'

'I will.' Whispered again, this time almost a prayer.

'Good,' Parker said. 'Let's drive to your house, you can get me that fax number and drive me back to my car.'

She nodded, and started the engine.

As they moved out of the diner's parking area, Parker said, 'This is an Infiniti.'

'Yes.'

'That means forever.'

'Yes.'

'Seems worth going for,' he said.

She nodded, not looking at him. 'Yes,' she said.

4

Jake's mobile home was all cleaned up. No dishes in the sink, no clothes on the bedroom floor, no newspapers on top of the water closet. Having knocked once and gotten no response, Parker had let himself in, the flimsy lock on this structure offering not much of a challenge, and now there was nothing to do but settle down and wait.

There were books on a living room table that hadn't been there before, most of them fantasies about life in medieval castles on other planets — the sister's reading, it must be. Parker took one of them, read for a while, then stopped reading and merely waited.

He had come here direct from the meeting with Elaine Langen, Dalesia's original note with his contact's fax number now in Parker's pocket. He had a couple of details to settle with Jake, which would have to be through the sister, and then he could go back to Trails End Motor Inne. And there wouldn't be much to do after that but wait for Briggs to get here, and then the armored cars.

Before they'd separated, Parker had reminded Elaine Langen once more about the handover at the stop sign on the night, while the armored cars were being loaded, when she would let them know which one carried the cash. That was the last piece, and it seemed to him that the woman was cowed enough just to do her job and not make any more trouble.

He waited an hour and a half, and got to his feet when he heard the key in the lock. The sister walked in, looking busy and preoccupied, carrying a plastic bag with a drugstore's name and logo on it. She saw him as she was closing the door, jolted, recovered, finished shutting the door, and said, 'Well. You specialize in scaring the life out of me, don't you?'

'I need,' Parker told her, 'for you to take a message to Jake.'

'Not big on small talk,' she said, apparently to herself. Crossing past him, she said, 'Let me put this stuff away. You want coffee?'

'No need.'

She went into the bathroom, came back out empty-handed, and said, 'I get it, we're not gonna be chums. Fine. What's the message?'

'Wait a minute,' Parker said. 'When was the last time you hung out with your brother?'

'Grammar school,' she said. 'Why?'

'You're here because he got shot,' Parker

said. 'You're not here to be a hostess or something. We're not gonna take tea together.'

She thought that over, nodding her head. 'You're right,' she decided. 'If Jake wasn't in the hospital, I'd never have met you in my life, and I wouldn't miss the experience.'

'That's right.'

'I have the idea,' she said, 'he was involved with you and your friends in something he shouldn't have been, and whoever shot him, I'm glad they did, because now he's out of it, safe in the hospital.'

'That's right,' Parker said. 'But he can still help.'

'Not to get on the wrong side of the law all over again.'

'He can't, in the hospital. But he can phone his motel, tell them we got another guy coming in a few days, same deal.'

'I suppose so,' she said, clearly not knowing what the deal was.

'And tell him, we won't try to get in touch with him until he's out of the hospital.'

'I'll tell him.'

'Fine.'

He turned away, but she said, 'Wait one second, will you?'

He turned back. 'Yeah?'

'There's something I want to tell you,' she said.

'Go ahead.'

She waited, frowning, then abruptly said, 'I don't like Dr Madchen.'

He watched her face. 'You don't like him?'

'He isn't Jake's doctor now, not while he's in the hospital, but he's hanging around anyway, and he's making Jake nervous, and now he's making *me* nervous.'

'In what way?'

'I take it,' she said, 'he's somehow part of what you people are doing, or connected with it somehow. And he's like the nerd kid who just wants to hang around with the big boys, only he drops hints like how it's really important to him that everything be OK and — '

'Hints?'

'Just to Jake, I think,' she said. 'But I mean, in my presence. I guess he figures, I'm the sister, it's safe. But he's a needy guy, and he makes me nervous.'

'Thank you,' Parker said. 'All of a sudden, he makes me nervous, too.'

'You'll talk to him?'

'Yes.'

'And I'll tell Jake what you said.'

'Good.'

She walked him to the door. 'This Dr Madchen,' she said, 'I don't mean he's a bad guy or a threatening guy or anything like that.

I just mean he's drawing attention to himself because he's so needy and uncomfortable.'

'I understand,' Parker said.

'So when you see him,' she suggested, 'use your best bedside manner.'

5

A mile from Riviera Park, the rearview mirror in the Lexus showed Parker a battered old tan Plymouth Fury that tugged at his memory. It seemed to be pacing him, hanging two or three cars back in moderate traffic as he drove east across Massachusetts toward the motel. Early afternoon, the thin September sun not yet low enough to obscure his view back there. Who was that?

Elaine Langen's house, when he'd gone there to get her gun. No other car parked outside when he arrived. The meeting with Mrs Langen cut short because a 'lady policeman' had come to the house. That tan Plymouth Fury parked next to his Lexus when he came around from the kitchen door and drove away.

So she recognized him, too. She was watching Jake's place, to see what activity might take place there, or she had beat cops watching it. For whatever reason, she connected this Lexus to both the Langen house and Jake's mobile home. And now she was following, waiting to see where he'd go next.

Nowhere with her. Parker made a few turns, accelerated, decelerated, put himself in positions where he could make abrupt turns across lanes of oncoming traffic, and without raising a sweat, she stayed with him. Sometimes she lost ground, but she never lost the Lexus.

He was just coming to the conclusion that the thing to do was find a railroad station. He could leave the Lexus, and take trains until he was alone, then rent a car and come back. But as he was thinking that, a graceful brown-leather covered arm — it reminded him of a ballerina's arm move, starting a lift — came out of the driver's door of the Plymouth and slapped a suction-cup red flasher on the roof.

No siren, but the flasher started its spinning crimson roll, and the bright beams of the Plymouth's head-lights flared alternately left and right, and she accelerated past the intervening cars — they dodged out of the way like rabbits from a coyote — and when she'd reached his rear bumper, a loudhailer voice, so distorted you couldn't tell if it was male or female, said, *'Pull over on the shoulder.'*

He did. The only ID he carried on him belonged to John B. Allen, and was safe. The registration in the glove compartment carried the name Claire Willis, who would be his married sister. There was no bad paper out on either name. If this cop didn't happen to find the Beretta clipped under his seat — and why should she? — there was nothing in the car to cause him trouble.

He stopped, crunching on the gravel shoulder, and ignored the gawkers as they crept by. Instead, he watched the rearview mirror.

She took her time in there. He could see her, on her radio. Checking the license plate, maybe arranging for backup, if it should turn out to be needed. But then at last she did come out, a tall, slender blonde woman in tan slacks and a short leather car coat, and moved forward toward his car.

A cop walks like a cop. Even the women cops do it. Women walk as though they have no center of gravity, as though they're all waifs, or angels, but cops walk as though their center of gravity is in their hips, so they can be very still or very fast. To see that kind of body motion on a woman was strange, particularly on a good-looking blonde.

Parker rolled his window down and looked out at her. Very good-looking. Sure of herself because she was a cop and because she was good-looking. And good at her work — Parker hadn't been able to lose her.

He said, 'Yes, Officer?'

'May I see license and registration, please?'

'Sure. Registration in the glove compartment. OK?'

She seemed surprised at the question. 'Get it, please.' He handed her the documents, and she studied them, saying, 'May I ask your occupation, Mr Allen?'

Fortunately, he remembered what he'd told Elaine Langen that time: 'Mostly,' he said, 'I'm a landscape architect.'

She raised a brow. 'Mostly?'

'Well, it's seasonal work,' he said, having no idea whether it was or not, but figuring she wouldn't know either. 'The rest of the year, I do other things. Or nothing. Depends how the season went.'

'This is your wife's car?'

'Sister. My Navigator's in the shop.'

'And have you had work up in this area, Mr Allen?'

'It's done now,' he said. 'It was just consultancy, for a Mrs Langen. I'm not doing the project. You want her address? I have it somewhere.'

'Not needed. Just wait a moment,' she said, and took his license and registration away to her car.

She was curious about him. She knew, from Elaine Langen's stupid move with the gun, from Jake Beckham, gunshot in a hospital — she knew something was in the air. And all of a sudden, she had the new guy in her territory, connected both to Elaine Langen and to Jake Beckham.

At this point, there was no way for the cop to get a handle on what was going down, but she was curious. She was going to poke; she was going to pry, and all because of Elaine Langen.

Two days. Two days from now this cop, and every other cop for five hundred miles, would know what was going down. Let them know. By then, it wouldn't matter. Not to Parker, anyway.

She came back. 'Mr Allen, I wonder if you'd open your trunk.'

'Sure,' he said, and got out and did so. He waited till she was shining her flashlight in at the trunk, empty except for a folded sheet of blue tarpaulin, and then he said, 'Is it all right to ask what this is all about?'

'Just a routine traffic check.'

He laughed at her. 'You've been dogging me for fifteen miles. I tried to shake you, and I couldn't.'

She looked at him, no expression. 'Do you consider yourself good at shaking cars pursuing you?'

'I guess not.' He shrugged. 'I never tried it

before, and it didn't work this time. But the thing is, Officer — '

'Detective,' she said. 'Detective Second Grade Gwen Reversa.'

'How do you do, Detective. The thing is, it's pretty obvious you're just after *me*, and since I don't know anything I'm in trouble for, I'm wondering how come.'

Instead of answering, she said, 'Thank you,' with a nod, meaning he could close the trunk; so he did, as she moved very slowly around the car, studying every inch of it. She was, he knew, looking for a violation, a broken light or something like that, so she could cite him and then possibly bring him in for further questioning. But there would be nothing to hook on to. He kept the Lexus clean.

Nevertheless, he realized, this car was through. When the detective finished her inspection, he would leave the Lexus, wiped down and key in ignition, in some store's parking lot where he could walk to a car rental agency. And when he got back to the motel, he'd phone Claire to report the Lexus stolen, get a rental of her own, and think about what car she'd want next.

It was with obvious reluctance that Detective Reversa gave him back his license and registration. 'Thank you, sir,' she said.

He nodded. He wouldn't ask her again,

because he knew she wouldn't answer. He said, 'Is that it?'

'Unless you have something you want to say?'

'Only, I'm glad I wasn't on my way to an important appointment.'

Her smile was cold. 'So am I, Mr Allen.'

She didn't follow him when he drove away from there, but she didn't have to. She'd picked up whatever information she was going to pick up, and she knew it. And Parker had picked up a couple of things, too.

For instance, she hadn't tried any names on him. 'How do you know Mrs Langen?' 'What's your relationship with Wendy Beckham?' 'Do you happen to know Jake Beckham?' 'What else are you doing in this part of the world, Mr Allen?'

She hadn't asked those questions. She should have, but she hadn't, and he knew that meant she knew he'd lied to her.

She was going to be a problem.

6

At dinner in the same family restaurant, Parker told the other two about Wendy Beckham's doubts about Dr Madchen. Dalesia said, 'I thought he was a jerk that first day in his office. Comes out with a folder, has to have a very important conference with the receptionist, at the same time he's giving us the steady double-o.'

'I don't mind if he's curious,' Parker said. 'I mind if he's drawing attention. This woman cop on the case, this Reversa, she's sharp, and she knows something's happening, and she's keeping an eye on everything that ripples anywhere around Jake.'

'So,' McWhitney said, 'you mean we should stop this guy from rippling.'

'He's seen Nick and me,' Parker said.

With a snort, Dalesia said, 'And he'll sure remember us.'

'A little later tonight,' Parker said, 'we'll go visit him and see if he can learn to control himself.'

'Good,' McWhitney said. 'Save me for if it has to turn mean.'

Dr Madchen's home address was in the local phone book, and when Parker and Dalesia got there at nine-thirty that night, the neighborhood was a surprise. 'He didn't get this from pushing pills,' Dalesia said.

It was true. This had to be one of the richest neighborhoods anywhere around here. Large old houses set well back from the road commanded acres of rolling lawns and many specimen trees and well tended hedges. The few cars visible down the long driveways were recent and expensive.

This was a hard place to move around in without being noticed. There was nowhere nearby to leave the car, and it wasn't a neighborhood where people did a lot of walking, particularly at night.

They were in Dalesia's Audi. Parker's new rented Dodge Stratus would stay mostly out of sight. The second time they approached the doctor's address, Parker said, 'Let me out, circle back for me. I'll see what's the situation.'

There was very little traffic along these curving roads, none of them major streets from anywhere to anywhere, just ribbons laid out on a field of emerald green. The tall streetlights were soft, and so were the private lights defining driveways and entrances. At the moment, there wasn't another moving vehicle in sight. Parker left the Audi and walked in along Dr Madchen's blacktop drive in a faint, pervasive amber glow that made everything visible but nothing easy to focus on.

The Madchen house was brick, probably a century old, three stories high. Elaborate white woodwork surrounded all the doors and windows, and a large, empty wooden porch crossed the front, looking as though no one had used it since the invention of air-conditioning.

Not trusting the old wood floor of the porch to be silent, Parker moved around the house to the right, where he saw lights in windows. Moving slowly but steadily, keeping a few feet back from the windows, he passed along the right side of the house.

First a living room, brightly lit but empty. Then a dining room, where a uniformed Asian maid finished loading a round silver tray with dinner things and carried it away through a dark wood swinging door. Then a smaller room with darker furniture and walls, and a blue-lit woman not quite facing the window Parker peered through.

He stopped. The woman was fiftyish, heavyset, with too-black hair. She was seated deep in a soft broad-cloth armchair, and wore a lumpy satin robe or muumuu with Hawaiian island scenes repeated on it. She was barefoot, her feet on a hassock. She gazed forward, discontented, brooding. The television set she glowered at, its sound rising dimly and disjointedly through the window, was out of Parker's sight, below and just to his right of the window.

He watched her for a minute. The Asian maid entered and asked something respectful, folding her hands at her waist like a character in a movie. Without looking away from the screen, the woman said something sour. The maid nodded, crossed to pick up the squat empty glass from beside her mistress, and carried it out of the room. The woman abruptly called something after her, still without looking away from the television set. Parker thought he made out the word 'ice.'

The maid didn't immediately return. Parker re-traced his steps back to the road. Three minutes later, when Dalesia arrived, Parker went around to the driver's side. When Dalesia lowered his window, Parker bent to say, 'He isn't home. Just a wife and a maid. Keep circling, I'll wait for him, see what we do.'

'Fine.' Dalesia nodded generally at the

neighborhood. 'You know,' he said, 'along about the second week, I bet this gets boring.'

★ ★ ★

An hour and a half later, a car came slowly down the road, its right blinker switched on. There was no other car anywhere in sight. This had to be the doctor.

Parker waited, leaning against the plump specimen tree shaped like a lollipop, with maroon leaves, that stood off to the left of the driveway, midway between road and house. The oncoming car's lights flashed over him as the car turned in, but he doubted he'd been seen. The doctor's night vision would be limited to what he expected to see along this well-known route.

As the car moved slowly toward the house, Parker stepped away from the tree and crossed the lawn to intercept it. The doctor, alone in the car, holding the steering wheel with both hands, was miles deep in his own thoughts and wasn't aware of anything else until Parker tapped his side window. Then he jolted away, slamming on the brakes, barely stopping himself from thudding his forehead against the windshield.

Parker patted the air downward: calm down. Then he lifted a finger: wait.

Dr Madchen stared at him in terror as Parker walked around the front of his Alero and got into the passenger seat. 'Back out of here,' he said.

'What are you — why is the — what are you — '

Parker tapped a knuckle on the doctor's kneecap; not hard, just enough to draw his attention. 'Back out of here,' he said.

'You're not supposed to — we're not supposed to know — '

Parker said, 'Well, this would be easier,' and brought the Beretta out of his pocket, not pointing it anywhere in particular.

'No! I don't want to die!'

'Then you'll back out of here.' Finally the doctor got the idea. Shaking, clumsy, he managed to shift the Alero into reverse and jump on the accelerator.

'Easy.'

'Yes. Yes.'

'Back around to the right and stop.'

The sight of the pistol had calmed the doctor wonderfully. He backed out of the driveway and around to the right, stopping along the low curb. There were no sidewalks here.

'Put it in neutral.'

The doctor did that, too, then turned a very earnest face toward Parker. 'I don't want to die,' he explained, as though there might have been some question.

'That's good,' Parker said. Bending down a bit, he saw, in the right side mirror, headlights approach. Putting the Beretta away, he opened his window and waved his arm. Dalesia drove by, and Parker said, 'We'll follow him.'

The doctor put the Alero in gear. 'I don't see — I don't see why — '

'We'll talk when we're all together.'

Dalesia drove them away from that expensive neighborhood, into the nearby commercial neighborhood that's always to be found in an area like that. It included an all-night supermarket, a glaring bubble of fluorescent light in the darkness. Dalesia turned in at the parking lot there, and the doctor followed. Dalesia parked some distance from the store, and Parker said, 'Stop to his left.'

'All right.'

'Shut off the engine.'

'I haven't done anything wrong.'

Dalesia got out of the Audi and slid into the back seat of the Alero. 'You've been a naughty boy,' he told the doctor.

The doctor twisted halfway around in the seat, face distorted. 'No, I haven't! I did everything Jake asked me to do, I'm willing to do *whatever*.'

'You're hanging around the hospital,' Parker told him. 'You don't have a job there.'

'He's my patient, I want to be sure.'

'He's not your patient now. You come in there,' Parker said, 'and you act like a little boy with a secret. You talk to Jake about what's happening — '

'No, no, I wouldn't!'

'You *hint* about what's happening. You hint in front of his sister. Who else do you hint in front of?'

'Nobody! No one! I swear, I wouldn't — I *need* this! I need it, you don't understand, the life I live, I need this, I don't want to die — '

'I got that,' Parker said.

'I don't want to die,' the doctor said, more calmly. This time, it was a humble statement, as though he were asking permission. 'If this doesn't happen,' he told them, 'this thing you two are doing, if this thing doesn't happen, I'm going to die.'

Parker watched him. 'You are?'

'I can't live. This is my last, you're my last hope.'

Parker and Dalesia shared a glance. Dalesia said, 'So you don't want to louse things up.'

'No! No! Anything but!'

Parker said, 'Stay away from the hospital.'

'I will,' the doctor said. 'I hadn't realized, but you're right, you're absolutely right, I — '

'Stay away from Jake,' Parker said.

'I will. I promise.'

'No more hints.'

'No.'

'No more hanging around.'

'No.'

'Not a word out of you to anybody.'

'No,' the doctor said, and sat up straighter, and crossed his heart and held his right hand up like a Boy Scout. 'I swear to God,' he said. 'Hope to die.'

7

From the rear of the Trails End Motor Inne, where Parker and the others had been placed by Jake Beckham, you could see and hear the MassPike, just to the south, beyond a chain-link fence and a wooded gully. The sound was undifferentiated rush, steady enough to become white noise, and the constant streaming by of toy-size vehicles was soothing to watch, in its own strange way. Most of the regular customers of the motel were around on the other side, facing the local road and the swimming pool, which was still open though too cold for anybody to swim. Their three rooms were not contiguous, but spaced apart half a dozen units or so, along the ground floor. This time of year, there were no customers at all upstairs.

The day after they'd cooled off Dr Madchen, in the middle of the afternoon, Parker sat in the open doorway of his room, looking out toward the MassPike, doing nothing but wait until tomorrow, when the work would be done. He'd been there for a while, empty and relaxed, when McWhitney drove slowly past in his red Dodge Ram pickup. He pointed at Parker, as though to say, don't move, wait for me, and Parker nodded. McWhitney went on, parking the pickup in front of his own room, then came walking heavily back to where Parker had now gotten to his feet.

'This woman cop of yours,' McWhitney said, by way of greeting.

'What about her?'

'Describe her to me.'

'Blonde, late twenties, good-looking, dresses well.'

'I don't know about the 'dresses well',' McWhitney said.

Where they stood, facing south, the MassPike a flat barrier wall in front of them, the thin September sun shone down at them from a slant. Parker turned away from it to look more closely at McWhitney. 'What do you mean?'

'I think she's tailing me,' McWhitney said.

'You? Why does she even know you?'

'That's the question in my mind, all right.'

'Where did you see her?'

'There's a town near here with a drugstore with a phone booth in it,' McWhitney said. 'A real phone booth, for a little privacy, I went there to check in with the guy who's taking care of my bar while I'm gone. On the way out, I noticed this woman, because she's the kind of woman you'll notice — '

'Sure.'

'And then,' McWhitney said, 'coming out of the drugstore, there she was, parked across the street, looking at a roadmap.'

Parker frowned. 'I'd think she was smarter than that.'

'Maybe she figures I'm not worth all her smarts. Anyway, I'm walking back to my truck, I see her, I remember seeing her before, and all of a sudden I'm thinking, wait a minute, I saw her before this, too. Before today.'

'You're sure it's the same woman.'

'Good-looking blonde, late twenties. Could be a cop, I suppose, how can you tell?'

'You can't.'

'No.' McWhitney scratched his head, looking aggravated. 'The question is, what's she doing bird-dogging *me*?'

'Makes no sense,' Parker said.

'With you there's a link,' McWhitney pointed out. 'She's got you through your car here, your car there. I'm not around any of this stuff, I showed up late. How come she made *me* all of a sudden?'

'I don't get it,' Parker admitted.

'Neither do I.' McWhitney glowered back at the sun. 'It's making me mad,' he said. 'But who the hell am I mad at? And for what? If somebody screwed up, who was it? Nick? You? But how would you even screw up?'

'I want to see this woman,' Parker said.

'Be my guest.'

'Drive out again. I'll come with you.'

'That links us pretty tight.'

'If she's tailing you,' Parker said, 'she's already linked us. I just want to see what she's doing, try to figure out why she's doing it.'

McWhitney considered. He was angry, and wanted to relieve his feelings somehow, but couldn't figure out how. 'Fuck it,' he said. 'Come along.'

Parker closed his room door and walked with McWhitney down the row of closed green doors, past his own Dodge and Dalesia's Audi to the pickup. He slid in on the passenger side, and McWhitney said, 'Anywhere in particular?'

'Do your drugstore run again.'

'Fine.'

They left the motel, and McWhitney took his time on the local roads, constantly checking his rearview mirror. 'I don't know where the hell she is,' he said.

'She'll show up.'

McWhitney stopped at a stop sign, took his time, looked all over the place, started through the intersection, then looked down to his left and said, 'Son of a bitch, there she is!

Parked down there, see? Here she comes.'

Parker looked past McWhitney's jutting jaw and saw the car down there pulling away from the shoulder, saw the blonde at the wheel. 'I see her,' he said.

'So?' McWhitney's belligerence was increasing, now that she was actually there, hanging discreetly back in his mirror. 'What do you think now?'

'Head back to the motel,' Parker said. 'I think you and Nick and I have to talk.'

McWhitney gave him a quick look. 'Why? Something wrong? What is it? Isn't that your cop?'

'No.'

'I give up,' McWhitney said. 'Do you know her? Who is she?'

'I've seen her,' Parker said. 'Her name is Sandra. She was a friend of Roy Keenan.'

8

'We don't need this,' Dalesia said.

'Well, we got it,' McWhitney growled. Now that he'd found out the one he should be mad at was himself, he sat hunkered, beetle-browed, as though waiting for a chance to counterattack.

The three sat in Dalesia's room, the door closed against the evening view of the MassPike. There were two chairs, flanking the round fake-wood table, and Dalesia and McWhitney sat there, each with an elbow on the table, while Parker stood, sometimes paced, sometimes stopped to watch one or the other face.

'That's a few hundred miles,' Dalesia complained. 'From Long Island to here. But you never saw her before today.'

'I think I did,' McWhitney said, and beat the side of his fist gently on the table. 'I think I probably saw her, maybe a few times. What do you think to yourself when you see that? 'There's a good-looking blonde'.' Not, 'There's the good-looking blonde I saw yesterday'. You aren't *looking* in that kind of way.'

Dalesia, as though grudgingly, said, 'That's true, I guess. Good looks can make a woman anonymous.' He grinned at McWhitney, apparently deciding to make nice. 'Anybody looks at an ugly beak like *you* two days in a row,' he said, 'they're gonna notice.'

Parker said, 'What does she want, that's the question.'

'Good,' McWhitney said, rather than have to answer Dalesia. 'You tell us. What *does* she want? She can't still be waiting for her partner to show up.'

Dalesia said to Parker, 'You saw her before, when Keenan braced you, but you didn't talk to her.'

'No, Keenan used her as a decoy to get me in position where he could suddenly show up. Then she left. He said her job was to be somewhere around, out of sight with a three fifty-seven Magnum.'

'Christ on a crutch,' McWhitney said.

Dalesia said, 'So that's what happened. Keenan went into Nels's bar, and this Sandra woman stayed outside as backup. Didn't help him much, but there she is.'

As though reluctant to say it, or to say much of anything, McWhitney told them, 'He had a walkie-talkie in his pocket.'

Parker said, 'But he didn't use it.'

'He didn't get the chance.'

Dalesia said, 'That was at night. What, around eleven?'

'A little earlier. That bar doesn't get a late-night bunch, not even on weekends.'

Dalesia said, 'All right. Whatever happened between you and Keenan happened that night. Then what? In the morning, you came out to look for me?'

'Yeah, I went to Stratton first, and got you from him. Told him I wanted to bring you in on a job.'

Dalesia laughed. 'You sure did.'

Parker said, 'When you leave there, does anybody else live in the building?'

'No, I've just got this guy comes in to open and close the bar, run the place. He's got a home to go to.'

'So when you left,' Parker said, 'this woman followed you until you landed somewhere, until she could leave you for a while, and then she went back and tossed your place. What did she find?'

'Nothing!' McWhitney looked as though he might get insulted.

Parker shook his head. 'Come on, Nelson,' he said. 'This woman's a pro, she's at least as much a professional as Keenan was. She went into your place when it was empty. She didn't have a lot of time because she had to get back in position behind you, but she spent a little time, and what did she find?'

McWhitney furrowed his brow, thinking. He wasn't thinking about what the woman had found; he was thinking about what he would say. 'All right,' he said. 'She found some patted-down dirt in the cellar. And she found some empty acid bottles. That's all.'

'She didn't find any walkie-talkies, any wallets.'

'I'm not a complete idiot,' McWhitney said. 'You want to find those things, you have to walk into Long Island Sound.'

Dalesia said, 'Parker, go back to your question. What does she want?'

McWhitney said, 'She wants to know what happened to her guy.'

'I don't think so,' Parker said. 'She knows Keenan is dead. She's not gonna be into revenge, or justice, or take care of your partner, or any of that. She's a pro. She's here because she wants something else.'

Dalesia said, 'Maybe she just wants to know what we're all up to.'

McWhitney, growling again, said, 'We all know what she wants. It's the same as ever. She wants Harbin.'

They studied that. 'The reward,' Dalesia said. 'It's still the reward. We're busy over here, and she's still working her agenda.'

McWhitney said, 'She thinks what's going

on, we're protecting Harbin. We think Harbin is in the past, she thinks he's in the present.'

Parker walked to the door, opened it, looked out, saw running lights now on the trucks streaming along the highway. He shut the door and said, 'We can't have her here when we're working.'

Dalesia looked at McWhitney, who nodded, then shrugged. 'I always think,' he said, 'it's a waste to kill a good-looking woman.' He shrugged again. 'But we live in a wasteful world.'

9

The phone rang. Parker opened his eyes, and the LED readout on the bedside clock radio read 2:17. The red numbers also gave enough light so he could see the phone. He unhooked it, put it between pillow and ear while he looked around to be sure nothing had changed since he'd switched the lights out, and said, 'Yes.'

It was McWhitney's voice: 'Your Sandra's here. She drew down on me. She wants a meet, the four of us. She says, don't bring a gun.'

'Of course I'll bring a gun.'

Sitting up, Parker kicked the crumpled newspapers away from the bed while he listened to McWhitney breathe and then say, 'Hold on.'

There were faint voices away from the phone in McWhitney's room, and then the clatter of the receiver being put down; and then a female voice, hoarse and impatient, said, 'If you carry it in your hand, I'll kill you. If you carry it in your pocket, what's the point?'

'I don't leave home without it.'

'If you make me nervous,' she said, 'it won't be good.'

He had nothing to say to that, and after a bit the receiver clattered again and then McWhitney said, 'I gotta call Nick.'

'I'll be there.'

★ ★ ★

Parker walked down the line of green motel doors. Off to the right, the running lights on the highway had thinned out but still drew a yellow-white-red scarf across the throat of the night.

Ahead of him, a door opened. He paused, but it was Dalesia coming out. He saw Parker, grinned, and said, 'The lady's taking things into her own hands.'

'I don't need this,' Parker said. Twenty-four hours from now, they would be waiting for the armored cars. No, Parker would be at the stop sign, waiting for Elaine Langen and the number of the truck they'd want.

'Nobody needs it,' Dalesia said, as they walked down the line together. 'But it's what we got.'

Dalesia knocked, and the door was opened by McWhitney. He was barefoot, wearing dark trousers with a white T-shirt hanging loose, and his expression was disgusted. 'Do you believe this shit?'

They entered, and the hard-faced blonde was seated at the round table, which she'd pulled back into the front corner opposite the door, leaving the hanging swag light to dangle over air. She wore black leather slacks and boots, a bright green high-neck sweater, and a black leather jacket with exaggerated shoulders. Her left hand was on the table, palm down. Her right hand held a pistol, loosely, pointed nowhere, its butt on the back of her left hand.

'Come in, gentlemen,' she said. 'I like you all over there.'

Meaning the diagonally far corner of the room, straight back from the door. They went over and stood in a row, leaning their backs against the rear wall of the room, the bathroom door immediately to their left, and the bed beyond it.

McWhitney said, 'OK, we're all here. Just say it.'

'I've got a mortgage,' she said, 'on a nice little house on the Cape. I'm helping to keep my friend's daughter in private school. I made good money with Roy Keenan, all in all, sometimes fat, sometimes thin, but now that's done.'

Dalesia said, 'You need another Roy Keenan.'

'As a matter of fact,' she said, 'I was always better than he was, and we both knew it. The way the business works, it was better for him to be in front. I'll find another front man, that isn't the problem. The problem is, the current job. I need it for my cash flow, before I can move on to something else, but there's been too much time wasted on it.'

McWhitney, surly and rebellious, said, 'What the fuck do we care about *your* problems for?'

'You made my problems,' she said. 'That asshole Harbin should have been in our kill jar weeks ago. There's no way for him to go that far out of sight and still be breathing. It's been obvious for a long time that one of you put him down and knows where the remains are, and that's all I need. I don't need to point any fingers, I just need to get this job off the books.'

Parker said, 'Why should we deal with you?'

'Because I've got dossiers on you,' she said. Pointing at McWhitney, she said, 'I can give the law very good reasons to dig around in that cellar of yours.' To the others she said, 'I don't have convictable stuff on either of you, but I have *interesting* stuff, and I have every one of you in the room where Michael Harbin was last seen alive. I'm pretty sure you were all in that room to plan a robbery that then didn't happen, for whatever reason, and I know damn well you're all hanging around in this place because you've got some other robbery worked out.'

She lifted the gun hand and waved it, not threatening but betraying impatience, rubbing away their misconceptions. 'I don't give a shit what crimes you people get up to,' she said. 'I know you're wide boys, and I want nothing to do with your play, including informing on you. When I saw yesterday, you two in the pickup truck, that you'd made me, I knew it was time to come talk.'

'God damn it,' McWhitney said.

She said, 'If you cold-shoulder me tonight, I'll walk away and I'll eat the loss, and I *hate* to walk away from time invested with no return. I hate it so much I'll turn in those dossiers just out of spite. And if you think you can take me down, my friend has the dossiers and you'll never find her, and she'll know what to do with them the day I don't phone in.'

Parker said, 'To find a dyke on Cape Cod with a daughter in private school and a canary-yellow-haired roommate would not be impossible.'

Quietly, Dalesia said, 'There's three of us and one of her and it's a small room.'

227

'No, fuck that,' McWhitney said. 'Wait a minute, I'm trying to think.' But then he frowned at the woman and said, 'Just to satisfy my curiosity, do you know why Harbin was wired?'

Parker said, 'What difference does that make?'

'I just want to know.'

'So that's what happened,' she said. 'Somebody did have a handle on him, and you people found the wire.'

Disappointed, McWhitney said, 'But you don't know why it was there.'

'No, I get it,' she said. 'I didn't know he had it on, but it makes sense.' She gestured a little with the gun. 'The state reward money on Harbin is for killing a trooper during the commission of a crime. The crime was smuggling, off the Jersey coast.'

'Drugs,' Dalesia said.

She nodded. 'That's what was coming in, from Central America, that's what made it state. What made it federal was, what was going out was guns. You know, down there the rebels and the drug guys are all mixed together.'

Parker said, 'That doesn't add up. If they wired him, they know where he is, so how can there be reward money out on him?'

'One of the things that helps guys like you,'

she said, 'is, the law is a lot of little competing offices. Turf battles. So one bunch got hold of Harbin, and for a while they'd rather run him than turn him in. *They* don't get the reward. And they know he's got to do what they want for as long as they let him walk around loose. Like wear a wire whenever there's a meet.'

'Turns out, they didn't do him any favors,' McWhitney said. 'Let me make you a suggestion. You go away for two days, just two days.'

'No,' she said.

Parker said to McWhitney, 'Why? What are you offering?'

'Take it easy,' McWhitney told him, and turned back to the woman. 'It happens,' he said, 'I know where Harbin is.' Hastily he added, 'I didn't kill him, I just want you to know that. It doesn't matter, but I just want you to know.'

'Noted,' she said. Clearly, to her it really didn't matter.

'But I know,' McWhitney went on, 'where he is. Take a powder out of here, lady, you're too distracting. Give me a place to reach you, day after tomorrow, I'll take you to where Harbin is. I'll point and say *there*, and then you go your way and I go mine.'

The woman considered, then shook her

head. 'You just want two days to try to find my friend.'

Parker said, 'No, McWhitney's right. We're busy. We're too busy to go looking anywhere tomorrow or the next day. But after that, we got all the time in the world.'

Dalesia said, 'Add two days to your cost time equation. A small percentage, right?'

Again she thought it over, and this time she frowned at McWhitney and said, 'The body's available. It isn't burned or at the bottom of the ocean.'

'There's probably some acid damage,' said McWhitney.

She shook her head. 'You and your acid. You going back to that bar, when you're done here?'

'Oh, yeah.'

She got to her feet. 'I'll get in touch,' she said. 'Don't come outside for a few minutes.' And she walked sideways to the door, watching their hands, and left.

McWhitney sighed. 'I sure hope it doesn't come down to her or me,' he said. 'I think I'd lose.'

10

The next day was Friday, and that night the bank would move, so the bank people would have the whole weekend to get everything into its new position. Which meant that today Parker and Dalesia and McWhitney would also make their move.

When the three went out for lunch in Dalesia's Audi early that afternoon, there were two guys in warmup jackets closing the pool, disassembling the ladders and the board while the clear water glinted a goodbye at the sunless white sky. When they came back, a little before three in the afternoon, a gray cover like a trampoline, its segments stitched together with thick seams, spread across the rectangle of the pool inside its low chain-link fence, and around back a Honda Accord, the same shade of gray as the pool cover, stood just beyond the rented Dodge.

Dalesia drove past it, toward his own room, and Parker saw that there was someone seated at the wheel of the Honda: Wendy Beckham. 'Something,' he said.

Dalesia looked at his rearview mirror. 'Something?'

'Jake's sister. I'll see what it is.'

Dalesia parked, and they got out, McWhitney saying, 'I don't want any more problems.'

'I'll tell her,' Parker said.

Dalesia said, 'We'll still be ready to go in ten minutes, right?'

'If not, I'll call your room.'

McWhitney said, 'I'm starting to wipe my room down now, and when I'm done, I want to go. I don't want to stand around with my hands in my pockets, afraid to leave a print somewhere.'

'I'll see what she wants,' Parker said, and went away from them, over to where Wendy Beckham had gotten out of her car and stood now on the concrete walk in front of it. She was looking past him at the other two, now going into their rooms, and she looked worried.

Parker said, 'A message from Jake?'

'A message from *me*,' she said, and now instead of worried she looked angry. 'Jake finally told me what's going on.'

'That was stupid,' Parker said. 'What did he do that for?'

'Because he noticed, very late in the day,' she said, 'that he's the one gonna be left holding the bag.'

He said, 'You want to talk out here, or in the room?'

'Out here,' she said.

'Because . . . '

'Because I'm here to tell you, the deal's off.'

He frowned at her. 'What deal's off?'

'The robbery,' she said. 'The armored car with all the cash from the bank. The bank, God help us, that Jake used to *work* for. You aren't going to rob it. You aren't going to take it.'

He said, 'Why not?'

'Because you're all staying *here*, at Jake's motel.' She was really very angry. 'He's still the same irresponsible clown he always was,' she told him. 'You people will go, you'll get away with it or you'll be killed by the guards in the armored car, but whatever happens to you people, *he's* in trouble again.'

'I don't see that,' Parker said. 'We aren't registered here, under any names at all.'

'Don't you think the maids will talk?' she demanded. 'Don't you think the people that work here already know there's something funny going on? Three guys staying here without management knowing about it, three guys disappear, all of a sudden three guys rob an armored car. No, they won't catch up with *you*, but how long will it take them to get *here*?'

'Doesn't mean anything,' Parker said. 'They might even think Jake had something to do with it, because he's an excon, but every ex-con in this part of the state will be under suspicion and so what? Jake's in the hospital, legitimately in the hospital. He doesn't know anything about anything. They can suspect whatever they want, but how are they gonna prove anything?'

'You're here, in his motel.'

'He doesn't know a thing about it. Somebody pulled a fast one while he was away in the hospital. Besides, it isn't *his* motel, he's on staff here, he's an assistant manager.'

She shook her head. 'The minute the police start leaning on people here,' she said, 'the truth will come out, and Jake will go back to jail, and the worst thing is, you *know* that.'

No, the fact was, Parker didn't care. Jake would find his own way out of the jam, or not. He said, 'It's too late to stop it. It's going to happen, so you better tell Jake it's time to start practicing his poker face.'

'I'll stop you,' she said. She was wide-eyed, body clenched with determination.

He studied her. 'How do you figure to do that?'

'I'll go to the police! I'll tell them everything, I'll tell them what you plan to do.'

Parker shook his head. 'I wouldn't have believed it,' he said. 'You're dumber than your brother.'

She was offended, but also involved. 'What do you mean?'

'There's one guy in this group,' Parker told her, 'that doesn't spend a lot of his time thinking things through. I could walk you down there to his room, knock on the door, have you tell him what you just told me, and he'd kill you right then. Wouldn't even think about it, just drop you.'

She blinked, but remained defiant. 'Well, I'm not telling him,' she said, taking a step backward, away from him and toward her car. 'I'm telling you, you're the one I know, and you're the only one I have to tell.'

Parker said, 'The reason it's better to tell me than this other guy is, I take a minute to think about it. I take a minute and I think, *what* is she gonna tell the cops? Does she know when or where or how we're gonna do it? No. Does she know who we are when we're at home? No. The only thing she can do is blow the whistle on her brother, so instead of *maybe* he's in trouble definitely he's in trouble, and you did it.'

He waited, watching her eyes, as she went from defiant to frightened to something like desperate. Then he said, 'You want to talk to the cops, go ahead. Don't worry about us. I gotta pack now. Goodbye.'

FOUR

1

Dalesia left the Trails End first, followed a few minutes later by McWhitney, and a few minutes after that by Parker, who drove out past the covered swimming pool just around the time Wendy Beckham sat down in the hospital room with her brother to try to figure out how to keep him out of trouble, now that Jake's bad companions had announced they were not going to cancel their robbery.

'I'm sorry I told you,' Jake said. He was sulky, and getting bored in the hospital bed.

'Unless I can think of something to get you out of this,' Wendy told him, 'so am I.'

And they sat together in grim silence. This was the first day Jake's leg was out of the sling and he could sit up normally, but he wasn't even allowed to enjoy that.

★ ★ ★

When Parker got to the old mill in West Ruudskill, Dalesia and McWhitney had already driven their cars across the old, littered concrete floor, lumpy and powdering beneath their tires as they circled around

239

rusted pieces of machinery, rolls of wire, moldering stacks of cartons, until they'd reached as deep into the building as they could drive. From the broad open entrance at the other end of the place, long since stripped of its huge metal sliding doors, they were invisible back here.

Now they had nothing to do until Dalesia would drive off to meet Briggs at the motel at six. The inside of the old brick building was colder than the outside air, so they went out a squeaking side door to the remains of an old iron bench on a concrete platform over the stream. There they sat or paced, and saw that the white sky was not going to clear today. Heavy cloud cover or even rain could only be an advantage to them tonight.

Across the way they could occasionally, not often, hear a passing vehicle approach and cross the bridge, but where they were, the bushes and trees screened them from the road, and they could neither see nor be seen.

This was a dead time, nothing to do. Even McWhitney didn't feel like talking, though at one point he did say, 'What do we do if your friend Briggs doesn't show up?'

'We go home,' Parker said.

McWhitney looked at him. He'd clearly been expecting some endorsement of Briggs. Not getting it, he realized he hadn't needed it. So he nodded, and looked out at the quick stream, and said nothing else.

★   ★   ★

While they were out there, in the last of the day's thin warmth, one hundred sixty miles to the east, in Chelsea, just north of Boston, behind an eight-foot-tall chain-link fence, four armored cars were finishing their prep. The company was Harbor Coin Services, and the cars had all been bought used and were then refurbished. They were all the International Navistar Armored Truck model 4700, more or less the standard of the industry. They had been manufactured in America in the late eighties or early nineties and were as good as ever. The reinforced metal box that was their reason for being did not weaken or grow old. The parts that did, the engines and transmissions and brakes and the rest of it, could be repaired or rebuilt or replaced, but the metal box remained solid.

Each car held a crew of three: a driver and a guard riding shotgun in the front compartment, and a guard with his own fold-down seat in the sealed-away rear compartment. A shatterproof glass panel between the two compartments could be slid open for communication, but otherwise the wall between front and rear sections was as thick and tough as the outer walls.

The four trucks, their bodies painted red and hoods black, went through the company car wash as the final step in their preparation for the night's work, and then lined up behind the chain-link fence, awaiting departure time. The twelve men of their crews had an early dinner, without beer or wine, and got to Harbor Coin Services at six-thirty, ready to roll.

★ ★ ★

At six-thirty, Dalesia got into his Audi and maneuvered it back out of the building, on his way to meet Briggs, who was supposed to arrive at the motel at seven. He would be taking over Dalesia's room, and then Dalesia would lead Briggs and his van back to the mill. An evening chill had settled in, so after Dalesia left, Parker and McWhitney moved back inside, sitting in the Dodge, Parker in front, McWhitney in back.

★ ★ ★

The four armored cars lumbered like costumed circus elephants out of the Harbor Coin secure area onto city streets until they reached the Northeast Expressway. They took that west, over the Mystic-Tobin bridge to Interstate 93, and then took 93 and 95 in the long loop south and west and north around Boston and up to Interstate 90, which would take them across the state. They couldn't make much time in this early part of the drive, because the Boston area roads were full, but once they got west of Newton, the traffic thinned out enough so they could get into a line in the right lane and do a steady sixty-five while all the traffic around them snapped by at eighty.

⋆   ⋆   ⋆

Dalesia came back at ten to seven, trailed by a dark green Ford Econoline van with Florida plates. Briggs, when he got out of the van, looked as fussy and dissatisfied as ever, but offered no complaints beyond saying, 'Long drive.' He was still neat, though, in white dress shirt open at the collar, a tan zippered cotton windbreaker hanging open, and dark gray work pants. He looked like an office-machine repairman.

Briggs and Dalesia and Parker had worked together some years before, in the failed job that had led Briggs to opt for retirement, but Briggs and McWhitney were now meeting for the first time. Dalesia made the introductions, and Briggs and McWhitney shook hands while eyeing each other with some skepticism. Both were generally dissatisfied people, in different ways, and couldn't be expected to take to each other right away.

★   ★   ★

While Briggs and McWhitney were sizing each other up, Wendy Beckham was leaving the hospital, fretful, no closer than before to figuring out how to save her brother from his own carelessness. And Elaine Langen was on her way from home down to the former bank headquarters in Deer Hill. Her husband had been there all day, working with Bart Hosfeld, the professional who'd been hired to be in charge of the move, but Elaine only had to be there for the part she dreaded most, which was the farewell dinner.

The Deer Hill branch would continue as a bank, a part of Rutherford Combined Savings, but it would now be a Rutherford bank branch in the old-fashioned marble space of the bank building's main floor. The former Deer Hill Bank offices upstairs would be rented to other concerns, one of which would pay for the right to rename the building after itself.

For tonight, however, a different kind of transition would be taking place. For tonight only, the marble hall of the Deer Hill Bank, with its high ceiling and glittering chandeliers installed back in the twenties, was going to be a banquet hall.

Caterers were even now wheeling in round tables, chairs, tablecloths, place settings for eighty, and a wheeled rostrum for speeches, and the branch manager's office tonight would be the caterer's base of operations, with warming ovens and portable refrigerators and many trays lined with canapés.

At eight tonight, old-line bank employees and important local citizens would gather in this original branch of Deer Hill Bank to say farewell to that bank and to watch it be eaten in one giant gulp by Rutherford Combined. Speeches would be made, maudlin and tedious. Promises would be made, never to be kept. Memories would be stirred with many boring anecdotes of the old days of Deer Hill and the sweet little bank that kept the town going through thick and thin, mostly thin. Elaine's father, Harvey, would be remembered in ways that would make him unrecognizable.

It was going to be absolute hell, but longer. Elaine took a Valium with scotch and drove south, telling herself that at least the *ending* of tonight's activities would be a surprise for those pompous bastards.

★   ★   ★

When Briggs opened the side door of his van, they looked in at five long, lumpy rolls of thin army blankets, tied in two places each with clothesline. In addition to those, looking like too-small body bags, there were three liquor cartons in there that had been opened and reclosed.

'Let me show you these things,' Briggs said, considering which one he wanted to bring out first, actually squeezing one to feel what was inside. Making his choice, he pulled it closer and started to untie the lengths of clothesline. McWhitney, sounding suspicious, said, 'These things aren't new?'

'Oh, no,' Briggs said. 'You'll never get a new one, they're much too controlled for that. They have to get out into the world, where they can be stolen and sold and lost and borrowed and mixed up in the paperwork.' Now unrolling the blanket, he said, 'These have all been reconditioned. I don't know if any of them has ever been fired, except maybe in practice. Mostly, you know, particularly when they're owned by governments, these items are mostly for show.'

The last of the blanket was rolled back, and there was the 84mm Carl-Gustaf. Fifty-one inches long, grayish-tan metal, it was blunt and unlovely, a thick length of plain pipe that flared out like a megaphone at the butt. There were two pieces of wood attached, one under the trigger guard and the other screwed to a metal strap near the front.

'You load it here,' Briggs said, and snapped open the cone at the rear, which was hinged to the left. 'It's all normal,' he told them, and shut the weapon again. 'There are three sights, open here, telescopic here, which I don't think you're going to need, and infrared here.'

'That we'll use,' McWhitney said. 'Let me heft the thing.'

'Of course.'

Briggs handed the weapon to McWhitney, who hefted it and said, 'Heavy.'

'Thirty-six pounds,' Briggs told him. 'Six pounds more with the rocket in it.'

McWhitney shook his head. 'I don't want to have to fire this thing more than once.'

Dalesia, grinning, said, 'It's all in the aim, Nels.'

McWhitney opened the butt again, raised the weapon to his face, and sniffed. Briggs said, 'It won't smell.'

'Oil,' McWhitney said.

'They're reconditioned,' Briggs told him. 'As I said.'

Parker said, 'What else have you got in there? The rockets are in those boxes?'

'Yes, but let me show you the rifle I got.'

Parker said, 'You said Valmets.'

'Yes, but I got something else,' Briggs said, feeling through the rolled blankets, making another choice. As he untied the clothesline, he said, 'The problem with the Valmet, I could only get the M-sixty, not the M-sixty-two, and you don't want that.'

McWhitney said, 'Why not?'

'The Finnish army, it's cold up there,' Briggs told him, 'they use thick gloves, so the M-sixty doesn't have a trigger guard. You don't want that.'

Parker said, 'So what are we getting instead?'

'The Colt Commando.'

Dalesia said, 'An American gun?'

'That's right, developed for Vietnam. It's a short version of the M-16, and it's light, and you won't be worrying about long-range accuracy anyway, so it's fine for you.'

Dalesia said, 'I've seen these before.'

'Sure you have.' Opening the blanket, Briggs said, 'The middle section is the same as the M-16, but the barrel's only ten inches instead of twenty, and the butt's only four inches long. There's an extender in the butt you can pull out to make it seven inches long if you're going to do shoulder-firing, which I don't think you are.'

McWhitney said, 'The front of the barrel is threaded. What's that for?'

'There's a lot of muzzle flash,' Briggs told him, 'because of the short barrel, so you can attach a four-inch-long flash hider on the front. You don't care about that, that's just for somebody who wants to keep his location hidden at night. This way, it's the shortest it gets.'

'I think we need to practice with these things,' Dalesia said. 'Not shooting them, handling them.'

★ ★ ★

As they unwrapped the rest of the weapons, some miles away Elaine Langen arrived at her party and was met by her husband's undisguised jubilation. 'It's a wonderful night, Elaine,' he said, standing there in a tux, which really did look very good on him. 'It's so much better to close this chapter with a grand party, don't you think, than some cold banker's farewell.'

'Oh, I think it'll be a cold bankers' party,' she said, and went off to find the bar.

A more subdued party, if perhaps more honestly joyful, was taking place three miles north of the former Deer Hill Bank, in a room at the Green Man Motel, where Dr Myron Madchen had brought his special friend Isabelle Moran and a bottle of champagne with which to toast the beginning of their new lives together, lives that were being fashioned for them this very night. Isabelle had brought the glasses, the Brie, and the crackers, which she opened while the doctor opened the champagne, very carefully, as he always did.

A little later, he opened Isabelle's clothing just as carefully, because she was still swathed in white bandage around her torso below the breasts, to give support to a two-week-old broken rib caused by the violent husband. The last broken rib he would ever inflict on Isabelle; they drank to that, too.

And then they made love, very carefully, the doctor choosing the positions with great delicacy so as not to interfere with the healing of her rib. He was considerate, and he was knowledgeable, and she was grateful, which she demonstrated in a number of ways.

★ ★ ★

Once the armaments had been unloaded from Briggs's van, Dalesia drew him a map to show the route back to Trails End Motor Inne, and Briggs shook hands all around.

'I'll be in touch,' Parker said.

'Good hunting,' Briggs told them all, then got into his van, backed away to where he could turn around, and drove out of there.

Everything was now on the concrete factory floor: the guns lying atop their blankets, the rockets and the Commando ammunition still in their liquor boxes. McWhitney stooped to pick up one of the Commandos and sight along it, aiming at the driver's door on his pickup. 'It would be nice,' he said, cheek against the metal of the gun, 'if they'd see these things and just fold the hand. Give it up. Open the doors, get out of the way.'

Dalesia said, 'Never happen. Everybody's gotta be a hero for just one second. Then they fold like a beach chair, but first they gotta make you go that one step too far. That way, they can think back on it without being embarrassed about themselves.'

'The only thing they can do that's really stupid,' Parker said, 'is try to shoot at us.'

'Shoot at *us*, you mean,' McWhitney said. 'You're gonna be in the police car.'

'It's still stupid,' Parker said.

251

In another room in the Green Man Motel, down the hall from Dr Madchen and his love, Sandra Loscalzo came in from her early solitary dinner and immediately switched on her scanners. She would now pick up any police radio transmission anywhere within twelve miles of here.

Those guys had wanted two days to finish whatever it was they were doing. She was interested in that. Without endangering herself, there might be a way to include herself into whatever was about to go down.

Sandra had once heard a definition of a lawyer that she liked a lot. It said: 'A lawyer is somebody who finds out where money is going to change hands, and goes there.' It was a description with speed and solidity and movement, and Sandra identified with it. She wasn't a lawyer, but she didn't see why she couldn't make the concept work for her.

In her room at the Green Man, among her scanners, the night blossomed with police calls. Prowlers, domestic disputes, drunken drivers, heart attacks, rowdy teenagers in parks and playgrounds, fights in bars. None of them were her three guys. Not yet.

★ ★ ★

The sequence at the Deer Hill Bank party was first cocktails and shmoozing until eight, then dinner, then the speeches. Elaine Langen got just drunk enough in the initial phase of the evening to have no appetite for the second, so she ate practically nothing of dinner. However, with the prospect of the speeches still out in front of her, she did keep on drinking.

★   ★   ★

Wendy couldn't be physically present in the hospital after visiting hours, but she could phone Jake and did, after tidying the mobile home and eating her frugal dinner. 'Jake,' she started, 'I've been thinking.'

'Don't,' Jake said. He'd been thinking, too, and every thought he had led directly to a dead end. A solid wall. A black hole.

'No, listen, Jake,' she said. 'You and me, we've had our differences over the years, but we're still brother and sister, we can still take care of each other.'

'Oh, yeah, I'm fine.'

'The first thing you don't want to do,' she told him, 'is that. No giving up.'

He made a face at the blank television screen. Maybe there was something he could watch there after all. 'Yeah?'

'What you want to do tomorrow,' she advised him, 'when they come around, you just deny everything.'

'That's what I figured to do. If they come around.'

'They will, Jake. And when they do, no matter what they say, no matter what anybody at the motel says, you just deny it all.'

'There's only two people at the motel,' he said, 'you know, that could be, whatever, and I trust those people.'

'You're a trusting man, Jake,' she said. 'That's a good quality in you, but sometimes it can get you in trouble. You know what I mean.'

'Let me go on trusting them, all right? As long as I can, let me go on trusting somebody.'

'You can trust *me*, Jake,' she said. 'Listen, this is a terrible thing that's happening, but if it has to happen this is a good time for it. I've got good money from the beast' — her unaffectionate term for her ex — 'and tomorrow morning I'll go out first thing and get you a lawyer. A good lawyer.'

'No, no, no,' he said. 'You don't do that *first*, then they wonder, how come you got a lawyer already before anybody came around?'

'Oh,' she said. 'All right. But as soon as you

need a lawyer, trust me, I can pay for a good one.'

'Thank you, Wendy.'

'Maybe he can do some sort of plea bargain for you,' she said. 'If you know useful stuff on those guys.'

'Useful stuff?'

'Jake,' she said, 'you want as little jail time as you can possibly — '

'I don't want *any* jail time!' His heart was suddenly pounding so loudly he could hear it in his ears, as though it were coming through the telephone.

'Well, we can hope,' she said. 'But just to look at the possibilities, you are going to get charged, Jake. I mean, let's be realistic here. You are gonna get charged.'

'Oh, Jesus.'

'We'll get you a good lawyer, you cooperate, we'll get you back out in no time.'

'Wendy, don't.'

'I'm staying right here, Jake. We'll see this through together. Get a good night's sleep now.'

'Yeah, sure.'

'Make them give you a pill. Jake? I mean it. Make them give you a pill.'

'I will,' he said.

'OK. We'll talk in the morning. Good night, Jake.'

'Yeah.'

He broke the connection, and he did ask for a pill, and they gave him one. Then he lay on his back in the dim room and stared at the ceiling.

Before this, he'd been worried. Now he was terrified.

★   ★   ★

Briggs spent half an hour in Dalesia's former room at Trails End, but felt restless and couldn't sit still. He kept walking around the room, opening the door to look out at the traffic rolling on the MassPike, going into the bathroom to critically inspect his face and conclude, yet again, that he didn't need to shave at the moment, and in general behaving like something caged in the zoo.

It was the job those three were on; that's what had agitated him. He'd been away from that business a long time, and he'd forgotten the rush it involved, the sense that, for just a little while, you were living your life in italics. You weren't really aware of it when it was happening to you, but Briggs had seen it in Parker and Dalesia and the other one, and he'd found himself envying, not the danger or the risk or even the profit, but that feeling of heightened experience. A drug without drugs.

Half an hour was all he could stand, and then he said the hell with it; he didn't have to stay here; he could do whatever he wanted. He wasn't even checked in, so he wouldn't have to check out.

He packed the stuff he'd unpacked thirty minutes earlier, wiped the room down just in case, left the card key on the bedside table, and went out to the van. His one bag went in where all the weaponry had been transported, and he got behind the wheel and headed south, taking an underpass beneath the MassPike. Forty-five minutes later he was on Interstate 95, which would run him down the entire U.S. Atlantic coast to Florida. He figured, when he grew tired, he'd find a motel. Maybe in Maryland.

★   ★   ★

Not long after leaving Trails End, Briggs had passed an upscale restaurant out in the country, where Detective Second Grade Gwen Reversa, her tour done for the day, was having dinner with her friend. These days, Gwen was dating a lawyer. Well, it beat dating a cop. Somehow, in your off-duty hours, you needed to be with somebody you could talk to who would understand your language, your references, your assumptions. That was why actors dated actors, doctors dated doctors, mathematicians dated mathematicians.

Gwen had dated a couple of cops, but male cops just couldn't seem to get up to speed when it came to independent women. They *would* open the door for you, if they had to break your leg to get to it. They would protect you; they would make your decisions for you; they would explain for you how the world worked; and it would never occur to them they were patronizing, condescending bastards who should count themselves lucky Gwen kept a lock on her carry sidearm when off duty. They would condescend even when talking about the job, as though a person of either gender could make it to detective second grade without knowing the first thing about the work she was doing.

So a lawyer was better than that. Barry Ridgely, criminal defense attorney, attractive, good dresser, forty-one, divorced, two kids in private school, no real bad habits. Gwen had, naturally, checked him out when they'd first started seeing each other, and he was fine. He liked good restaurants, and so did she. He liked shoptalk, and so did she. It was just fine.

Tonight, Gwen's shoptalk was all about the man whose name, she was pretty sure, was not John B. Allen. 'He just didn't look right,' she said, not for the first time. 'You know how people look right in their jobs, or they don't look right?'

'I know what you mean,' Barry said. The restaurant was half full but quiet, dim-lit, comfortable. He said, 'I got a guy right now, veterinarian, strangled his wife. He *looks* like a veterinarian, you know? Caring, easygoing, patient.'

'But he strangled his wife.'

'She wasn't a pet. I tell you, Gwen, if I could bring a puppy into that courtroom, I'd get my guy off in a New York minute.'

Gwen laughed and said, 'Let me tell you about my landscape designer.'

'Oh, sure,' he said. 'Sorry, didn't mean to interrupt.' Which was one of the many nice things about him.

'That's OK,' she told him, because it was. 'I love the image of the puppy in court. But *my* guy, in the Lexus, is no landscape designer. You look at him, he could be a prison guard, he could be a mine worker. He isn't outdoors, he isn't saying, 'Put the petunias over there.' He just isn't.'

Barry nodded. 'Then why'd he say he was?' he asked, and put some monkfish in his mouth so he wouldn't interrupt her any more.

'He was at Elaine Langen's house when I

interviewed her,' Gwen told him. 'Not in the house, outside it. I didn't see him then, but that's when I saw his car, the Lexus. She's the one said he was a landscape designer.' She stopped, considering that. 'That's right, *she's* the one lied first, then he told the same lie when I stopped him, later on. And since then he's disappeared, I asked some people on the force, unofficially, you know, keep an eye out for the Lexus, it hasn't been seen since.'

'You said it was Jersey plates,' Barry pointed out, and poured them both some more chardonnay. 'Maybe he went home.'

'Or maybe he's lying low,' she said. 'If he isn't a landscape designer, and I know damn well he isn't, then what's he doing here, what's he doing with Elaine Langen, and why are they both lying about it?'

'Hanky-panky?'

'No,' she said, sure of that. 'She would, with anything in pants, but not him. He's a cold guy. With me, when I stopped him, he wore this affability like a coat, it wasn't him.'

'The cloak of invisibility,' Barry suggested.

'Exactly. Who knows who he is, down in there?'

'Well, if he's still around,' Barry said, 'and if he still has something to do with Mrs Langen, you'll find him.'

'Is he connected to my gunshot victim? I

wonder,' Gwen said. 'You know, the guy I told you about in the hospital.'

'A former boyfriend of Mrs Langen.'

'Who may have shot him, I don't know yet. But she and this Allen guy.' Gwen shook her head. 'I just have the feeling, whatever those two are up to, and it isn't hanky-panky, it would be very interesting to find out.'

'You'll find out,' he told her. 'I know you, you're a bulldog.'

'Thanks, Barry,' she said, grinning comfortably at him. 'Tell me about this veterinarian of yours. Why'd he strangle his wife?'

★   ★   ★

A little north of where they sat, in the restaurant that was only a restaurant for tonight, Elaine Langen, having not eaten her dinner and not drunk her coffee, but definitely having drunk her scotch and her wine, saw that the speeches were about to begin, and murmured to her husband, Jack, at her left hand, 'Liddle girls' room.' She stood carefully, so as not to stagger, and walked in more or less a straight line out of the room, out of the building, and into her car.

* * *

As Elaine was slipping shakily into the white Infiniti, Parker and Dalesia and McWhitney were getting into Dalesia's Audi and driving, at first with parking lights only, slowly out of the factory building and away along the road in the opposite direction from where they would meet the armored cars later tonight. Their goal was a diner down near the MassPike, where they could have their dinner in guaranteed anonymity. They reached the diner, and as they drove into its parking area, the four armored cars from Boston rolled by unseen up on the Pike, slowing for their exit just ahead.

* * *

A few minutes later, when the armored cars turned in at the entrance to the Green Man Motel, their headlights cut short the goodbye kiss of Dr Madchen and his Isabelle, who whispered hurried endearments, got into their separate cars, away from the headlights of all those trucks, and drove away to their for-the-moment homes.

The twelve crew members from the armored cars were booked into six rooms. It was nine-thirty now, and their escort would pick them up at one in the morning to lead them to the bank. In the meantime, they could shower, watch television, play cards, visit together, even nap. And when they did leave here at one o'clock, their traveling kits would stay in the rooms because they'd be coming back here once the move was finished, to get some real sleep before heading back east late tomorrow morning.

★ ★ ★

During the lead time before the robbery, Dalesia had been the man on the ground, learning the routes, finding places like the diner where they were eating now, and choosing the vehicles they would use tonight. Now, after they'd finished and paid, they got back into the Audi, and Dalesia led them first to the civilian car they would drive instead of one of their own. 'It's a wreck,' he told them, 'but it runs. At least it'll run as long as we need it.'

The used-car dealership he drove them to, just east of Rutherford, did not boast cutting-edge-security on its premises, but then, it didn't have cutting edge in its goods for sale either. This was not an operation connected with a new-car dealer, selling pretty good trade-ins, but a small private guy whose stock consisted of clunkers waiting for their fourth or fifth owner, and meantime lined up in gloomy rows under flapping pennants.

Two floodlights atop the trailer used for an office were the main deterrent to thieves, but Dalesia ignored them, pulling onto the lot and stopping in front of the trailer door. Illuminated by the floodlights, he twisted around to hand a key on a cardboard tag to McWhitney in the backseat, saying, 'The first time, I picked my way in, but then I found an extra key to the front door in the desk, so here it is and just leave it. Top drawer.'

'Good.'

Next, Dalesia gave McWhitney a small piece of notepaper from Trails End Motor Inne, saying, 'When you get in, on your left, there's a keypad. The number's two-eight-five-seven. He's got that in his Rolodex under 'Alarm.' The car key you want is on hook seventeen, for that Chevy Celebrity back there. And this is your route from here back to the factory.'

'See you there,' McWhitney said, and got out of the Audi.

They waited until he'd entered, stepped inside to disarm the alarm, and stepped back out to wave that everything was OK, and then Dalesia drove them away from there, southeast. Along the way, he said, 'The situation with this police car, this is the wrong season for it. It's in a very dinky little town, this time of year they don't have a police force at all. I broke into their town hall to check them out, and they've got two retired cops come in the beginning of December and play police department until the middle of March. It's because they're right next to the base of a ski area, so all of a sudden the joint's jumping. The rest of the year, the police car's kept in a separate little garage out behind the town hall.'

'But it looks like a police car,' Parker said. As they drove, he was changing into the hat, shirt, and jacket of a police uniform.

'It *is* a police car, Tootsie Roll on top, the whole thing. You'll see.'

*   *   *

It was a twenty-minute drive to the garaged police car, during which time, at Deer Hill Bank, the last of the invited guests finally trailed away, leaving Jack Langen and the hired security guy, Bart Hosfeld, and the other people in charge of tonight's big move. 'Time to start bringing everything upstairs,' Bart said, and the moving company people, who'd been waiting outside for nearly half an hour, came in to start the move. Every piece of paper from the downstairs vaults had been boxed and labeled, and now the boxes would be brought up to bank level and stacked near the front door, to make the transition as rapid as possible once the armored cars arrived.

★   ★   ★

At the hospital, the pill they'd given Jake had taken effect, but it had to fight a very troubled mind. Jake was groggily asleep, harried by bad dreams, never sinking all the way down into real rest. He argued with his dreams, fretfully, inconclusively, and some of the argument surfaced in muttering, low, distressed phrases that nearly made words.

★   ★   ★

The police car, which looked exactly like a police car, was twelve years old and had only forty-three thousand miles on it. It was a little stiff at first, but then smoothed down. Parker turned on the police radio to listen to the night as he drove toward the intersection where the job would go down.

★   ★   ★

In her room at the Green Man, Sandra Loscalzo also listened to the night, and it seemed to her that something unusual was going on out there. Every once in a while, there'd be a directive or a report that didn't appear to contain a subject, and she was beginning to believe they were all on the same subject:

'I've finished running Route Eleven. Everything clear.'

'Be sure you're in position to control the traffic light in Hurley when the time comes.'

Things like that kept snagging her attention — the glimmerings of some sort of movement in the night, like a whale too far below your ship to see. Something was starting up out there. Was it connected to her three guys?

★ ★ ★

There was one more vehicle for Dalesia to pick up tonight, the truck they'd transfer the goods to. This truck couldn't be stolen, because they'd have to use it more than once after the robbery, so Dalesia and McWhitney two days ago had taken the MassPike west to Albany, New York, and rented a truck, McWhitney using his legitimate business credit card from his bar. It had been stashed since then in the municipal parking lot in Rutherford. Now, after delivering Parker to the police car, Dalesia drove to Rutherford, left the Audi in the truck's place, and drove the truck to the factory.

McWhitney was already there with the Chevy Celebrity, a car about as old as Parker's police car but which had gone through a much more strenuous life. It was dinged and scratched and dented all over, and the muffler sounded like a bad case of asthma, but it ran.

McWhitney had all four of the Celebrity's doors open, so its interior lights illuminated to some extent the area around the car. Too much light might attract attention, which they didn't want.

When Dalesia got out of the truck and joined him, McWhitney was studying the Carl-Gustafs and their rockets in this soft light. Looking up, he said, 'I never loaded one of these things before.'

'If they were that easy to do wrong,' Dalesia said, 'they wouldn't sell them to so many third-world countries.'

'That sounds good. I'll watch.'

'Sure,' Dalesia said, and armed the weapons with self-confident speed.

Watching him, McWhitney said, 'Parker in place?'

'Just waiting,' Dalesia said.

'Like all of us.'

* * *

And like the armored car crews, all of whom were ready by one, when a police escort came to lead them to the Deer Hill Bank.

The five engines made enough noise pulling out of the parking area that Sandra went to the window and looked out. A whole lot of armored cars? Going where? Too late to get out to her own car and follow them. She went back to her scanners.

* * *

At one-thirty, when the moving men were just starting to load the four armored cars, under the direction of Jack Langen and other bank officials, separating files from commercial paper from cash, Dalesia used McWhitney's pickup truck to leave the factory and go meet Elaine Langen and get the number of the armored car that they would want. And an hour later, Dalesia drove fast into the parking lot of the diner at the intersection where the robbery was to take place, and where Parker

269

was waiting in the police car, because anybody who saw a police car behind a diner late at night would just assume the cops were cooping.

Parker saw the pickup drive in, and was out of the police car before Dalesia had stopped. Dalesia called out his open window, 'Didn't show! The damn party at the bank's over, Parker.'

Parker got into the pickup. 'I'll direct you to her house,' he said, and removed the police hat and jacket along the way.

When they reached the Langen house, it was completely dark. There was a door at the end of the multi-car garage, with a window in it. They smashed the window, unlocked the door, stepped in, and the white Infiniti was there. They moved fast through the dark house, up to the second floor, found her room, switched on the light, and she lay on her back on the bed, asleep, dressed except for shoes.

'Wha?' she said, blinking, lifting her arms to protect her eyes. 'Wha?'

'Up,' Parker told her. 'Fast!'

'Oh, my God!' She sat up, horrified. 'I forgot!'

'You got drunk. On your feet. Now!'

'I will, I will, oh, I can't believe I — '

Wailing, she hurried away into the

bathroom, and seven minutes later she was moving fast down the stairs with them, saying, 'The maid sleeps way in the back, she won't hear a thing.'

'You just go there and out,' Parker said.

'I can't go back there for just one minute.'

They all went through the house to the garage, Parker saying, 'Make it three minutes.'

'Five tops,' Dalesia said.

'Oh, God. I never thought I'd do a — It was the stress, it was my father's — Oh, never mind.' Distracted, she triggered open the garage door. 'I don't know why I'm explaining myself.'

'We'll follow you.'

Driving back toward the bank, seeing those headlights well back but constantly there in her rearview mirror, Elaine cursed herself for a fool. Everything she did was wrong. Shooting Jake, for God's sake! Getting drunk and forgetting what she was supposed to do tonight, and for *those* people.

With a wince every time her eyes saw those headlights, small, sharp, accusing, she thought, what if they didn't come after me until it was too late? It isn't too late now, I can make up for it, but what would they have done if I'd spoiled the whole thing? They would not have let me live, she assured herself. They would not have let me live.

I want to get away from here. But not that way.

But she had another chance; she could still do it right. She'd go to the bank; she'd tell Jack she'd gone home for a nap but really wanted to see at least part of the big move, so here she was, back. She'd make chitchat for a few minutes, find out which armored car would contain the cash, and then plead tiredness, say she'd seen enough to get the general idea, and leave. Pausing next to that pickup truck.

She had just made out the lights and activity spilling out of the bank, far ahead, when the headlights behind her clicked off. She drove on, more and more slowly, and saw that the scene in front of the bank was of constant ordered activity, brightly illuminated. In order not to disturb the neighbors more than necessary, the lights had been set to shine toward the area in front of the bank but nowhere else, so it was a white cone of busy movement up there, surrounded by the blackness of this moonless overcast night, as though it were a scene on stage.

The parking spaces near the bank were all taken, by the armored cars and state and local police cars and vehicles belonging to the bank executives and the moving people and the private security firm. Elaine drove slowly by, seeing the blue-coveralled moving men coming out, pushing dollies on which the cardboard boxes rode. Bank employees with clipboards directed each dolly to the appropriate armored car. The back doors of the armored cars stood wide open, and all four cars, it seemed to Elaine, were already at least half full. So she hadn't had much extra time to make up for her stupidity.

Slowly she rolled on by, and saw a dolly with a gray canvas bag on top of two boxes as a mover brought it to a stop behind the second armored car. More canvas bags were visible inside there.

Canvas bags were used for coins. This was the money car.

Elaine drove on by. On the driver's door, as she passed it, were black, squared-off digits: 10268.

'One-oh-two-six-eight,' she whispered, and drove on, speeding up slightly. At the corner she turned right, and then at the next corner and the next, and then left, mouthing the five numbers over and over the whole time. A minute later, she angled into the left lane on the empty street to stop next to the pickup truck. 'One-oh-two-six-eight.'

* ★ ★

In the hospital, the pill Jake had been given had begun to weaken, but his turbulent brain had not. Closer and closer he came to real consciousness, though he didn't want it. He wanted to be unconscious forever, but his brain wouldn't let it happen.

Sandra Loscalzo listened to her scanners and studied her maps of Massachusetts. Unfortunately she didn't have a detailed atlas of the state, and the road maps she did have wouldn't show every minor road, but from what she was hearing out of the night, the *thing*, whatever it was, that was happening or going to happen, existed along a line that ran north and south, roughly from a town called Rutherford in the north to a town called Deer Hill in the south.

Neither of these towns meant anything to her. She had come to this part of the world in search of Michael Maurice Harbin, and this was clearly something else entirely. But something interesting.

Carrying one police scanner in its vinyl bag, plus her own leather shoulder bag with the .357 automatic in it and the best of her roadmaps, she left her room at three in the morning and went out to see what there might be to see. Rutherford seemed the largest town in the area. She'd start there.

★   ★   ★

Dalesia dropped Parker off at the police car, then drove back to the factory, where McWhitney had the weaponry already placed in the Celebrity, some in front and some in back. Dalesia drove the Celebrity; McWhitney sat in back, one palm resting on a Carl-Gustaf.

★   ★   ★

Sandra saw the police car behind the diner as she drove by, but thought it was empty. The next police car she saw contained two uniforms and was parked at an intersection with a traffic light in a very small town called Hurley.

★   ★   ★

I got to get out of here, Jake told himself, and when he realized he must be awake, he found he was sitting up, moaning slightly and moving his torso slowly left and right. It wasn't bright in here, but he squinted as though it were. His whole head ached horribly, as though a clamp were being tightened around his skull. And he knew he had to get out of here; he had to get away; that was the only thing he knew.

He had not been on his feet since the shooting, but now he pushed himself off the bed and stood, tottering, bent forward, trying to find his body's balance through the screaming ache in his head.

He shouldn't have been able to walk. But the medicines he'd been given worked to combine now with the intense level of anxiety in his brain to short-circuit the pain signals his wounded leg tried desperately to send him, those lightning strokes of pain blurring and muddying before they could capture his attention.

He had too little strength in that leg now to accomplish a lot, but at least he could force himself to move. And did.

A door, in the right corner of the room. Would that be a closet? Would his clothes be in there? He wore only a two-piece blue-and-gray vertically striped pair of pajamas. He was barefoot.

Thinking hard about his balance, he moved away from the bed and toward that closed door. The knob was very hard to turn, the door much heavier than he'd expected, but yes, it was a closet. That was his zippered windbreaker hanging in there, and those were his shoes on the floor. No pants, which must have been messed up in the shooting.

He didn't care. Holding on with both hands to the bar in the closet, concentrating, he stepped first his left foot and then his right foot into the shoes. Then he took the windbreaker off its hanger.

No. That was impossible. He had to clomp back over to the bed, the shoes feeling like alien weights on his feet, and sit on the bed again before he could put the windbreaker on and zip it up. Then, standing again, he crossed the room to the partly open hall door, looked outside at an empty hall, and went out.

It was really very late at night. There were no people moving around in the halls. Two nurses sat at their station near the elevators. He moved in their direction, trying to think how he could get past them and down the elevator without being seen, and on his left he passed a door marked STAIRWAY B. He went just beyond it, then stopped.

He couldn't take an elevator. They'd see him here, and they'd see him on the ground floor. Could he go down the stairs? He was very weak and shaky; his balance was still unreliable. But how else was he going to get out of here?

The door to stairway B was one of the heaviest things Jake had ever in his life tried to move. It opened inward toward the stairs, so he could lean his weight on it and at last get it open enough so that he could slide through.

And here was a metal stairwell, and metal stairs going down. Jake looked at them, and a wave of dizziness made him drop back, leaning against the closed door behind him.

Only one thing to do. He sat on the floor and inched himself forward until his feet were over onto the first step down. Then he used hands and feet to move his torso down onto that step. And then the next step, and the next.

It turned out, he'd been on the third floor. It took a long time to get down all those steps, but after a while he found a rhythm in it, and he could just blank his mind and keep moving.

To the bottom, where he made it to his feet again and found another impossibly heavy door. Once again he forced his way through, and came out to one side of the main waiting room. Two of its walls, to his left and ahead, were glass in the upper half, on his left showing the admissions desk, straight ahead a side view of the front entrance. There were people in their own glass-sided room beyond the admissions desk, but none looked over here.

Jake kept to the wall and moved slowly around the room till he reached the next heavy door, this one mostly glass. He pushed through it and moved to the entrance, which was a revolving door, and even that was heavier than it should have been.

But he made it, around and out, and slowly but steadily walked away into the cool night air. No stars, no cars, no people. Just Jake, getting away. Everything would be all right now.

★   ★   ★

As the armored car crews climbed into their vehicles, shutting the rear doors, Jack Langen stood beaming in self-satisfaction on the sidewalk. What a night, what a beautiful night. As he stood there, Bart Hosfeld from the security company came over with his own broad smile and said, 'So far, it goes down like cream.'

Nodding at the last of the armored cars, Jack said, 'That's the only one I'm really worried about. All that commercial paper, bonds. What a nightmare to lose that.'

Bart said, 'Really? Not the cash?'

'Well, the cash, too,' Jack agreed, 'but not

as much. From the minute we knew this move would take place, we've been cutting back the cash at this location, not adding to it. It's still a lot, but not as much as it was.'

'Well, it's all going fine,' Bart said. Looking around, he said, 'I wanted to say good night to your good wife.'

'Elaine? She left hours ago. Before dinner ended.'

'Really? I could have sworn I saw her car, not an hour back.'

'She's long since asleep,' Jack said, and smiled. He preferred to think of Elaine asleep.

*   *   *

As the line of armored cars moved away from the bank, preceded by one private security car and followed by another, Dalesia and McWhitney arrived in the Celebrity at the intersection. They saw the police car but went on by, started out the road to the right, stopped, and reversed around in a half turn on the shoulder of the road. The right side of the car now faced the intersection.

*   *   *

Sandra had noticed several police cars stopped along the route she'd taken north, but she'd reached Rutherford without seeing anything actually happen. She'd decided to retrace her steps south when she heard, from the scanner on the seat beside her, 'They're on their way.'

Oh, really? Sandra made a U-turn and headed fast toward Deer Hill.

★   ★   ★

Jack Langen and Bart Hosfeld and a few of the others who would have work to do tonight at the Rutherford end of the operation left in a short caravan of vehicles, taking a different route from the armored cars, faster in some ways and more direct, but through built-up areas that were too chancy for the transport of the bank's assets. Driving along, listening to a Frank Sinatra CD, at moments even singing along, Jack thought to himself that today, tonight, he had at last completed the first step in separating himself from what he now liked to think of as the first Mrs Jack Langen.

The first one bought me, he thought. The second one I'll buy. 'It was a very good year.'

★   ★   ★

As she waited for the red light to change at Hurley, Sandra saw one of the uniforms get out of the police car stopped there and go over to the pole containing the control panel for the traffic light. It switched to green before he got there, but he unlocked and opened the door anyway, as Sandra drove on.

It was happening now. Whatever it was, it was happening. She remembered the various police cars she'd seen along the way, and then she remembered the first one she'd seen, silent and dark behind a diner, and this time it struck her as strange. That would be just ahead now, wouldn't it? All the other police cars tonight were out and obviously waiting for something. That one had been . . . hiding?

Ahead of her was the very intersection, and vehicles were just coming into it from the other direction. Sandra slowed when she saw what they were. First a white car with yellow and red words and symbols on its doors and hood and a warning light unlit on its roof. Then a large, square red box of an armored car, with a black hood. And another one behind it. And another.

This is it. She knew it; this was what was happening tonight. And was this what those three friends of Mike Harbin were involved with?

Sandra slowed almost to a stop. The first car passed through the intersection and continued, coming this way. The first armored car followed it across the intersection. Two more were behind it, in the intersection, and now a fourth was visible, behind the third.

Sandra was trying to see if there was a fifth armored car, and wondering what all these armored cars would be used for, when all at once flashes and explosions erupted from the darkness on the left, and then more explosions happened at the armored cars themselves. The whole engine compartment of the first one exploded into the air, raining chunks of black metal, and at the same time the same thing happened to the fourth in line, throwing the whole intersection into a sudden garish glare.

Sandra slammed on the brakes. She stared, amazed, as the lead car slued around, trying to get back, and men tumbled out of the lead armored car and, simultaneously, another flash and explosion on the left met an explosion onto the third armored car as lights suddenly flashed behind the diner, white lights and red lights, and, siren screaming, the police car came tearing out from behind the diner to slide to a stop next to the only armored car that hadn't been hit.

An amplified voice from a loudspeaker in the police car ordered, 'FOLLOW ME. DON'T STOP; FOLLOW ME.' And the police car veered away, the driver's uniformed left arm out his window, urgently gesturing at the armored car to follow. Which it did, lurching rightward, then hurrying off after the cop and away from its maimed companions, while Sandra thought, that's not right. There's something wrong about that.

The lead escort car had given up trying to get around and past the burning wreckage of the first armored car, and now brown-uniformed men came crowding out of it, guns in their hands. The armored car crews, having escaped from their destroyed vehicles, wandered in a daze or sat on the asphalt in the middle of the intersection, holding their heads. Sandra watched it all, glaring and distorted by the light of the three flaming trucks, and suddenly thought, it's a fake. 'It's a phony,' she said out loud. 'The police car's a phony!'

She had to tell them; she had to let them know. The story isn't *here*, with these blocked roads and burning trucks and dazed people. The story just went away with the only armored car that wasn't hit. Get after that phony cop. She actually had her hand on the door handle, shifting her weight to get out of the car, when she thought again. Wait a second. Whose side am I on here? If those *are* my three guys — and who else could they be?

284

— I don't want them arrested, I don't want them in jail. That way I'd *never* get the proof I need on Mike Harbin.

Keep going, fellas, she thought, as she put the car in reverse and U-turned backward away from there. Keep going, and I'll see you in a couple days.

Quickly the fires shrank and then disappeared from her mirror.

2

Parker spun the wheel hard right, pounded the brake, and the police car skewed around to a juddering stop, crossways on the road. He jumped out to the asphalt, looked over the car's roof at the oncoming armored car, and put both arms up over his head, waving them back and forth to tell the driver to stop. He could see the driver plain in his dashboard lights, hunched so far forward over the wheel, his nose nearly touched the flat glass pane of the divided windshield. Beside him, the guard was shouting into a microphone with a spiral black cord.

The driver hit his brakes, pushing himself back from the window with one hand, then waved his own arms, asking Parker in dumb show what he was supposed to do next. Parker pointed at him and then at the roadside, telling him to get out of there, but the guy firmly shook his head. He knew he was supposed to stay with his vehicle.

But then he twisted around, staring backward, and so did the other guard, so the one in back must have seen Dalesia and McWhitney coming. Yes, now Parker did, too:

the two running forward from where they'd left the Celebrity behind the armored car, Dalesia on the driver's side, McWhitney on the other. Both now wore white hooded sweatshirts with the hood up over their heads and forward beside their faces, and both had on deeply black sunglasses with very large lenses. Both ran with the Colt Commandos held in front of their chests at port arms.

The driver put his engine in gear, and the armored car lurched forward as he labored the wheel around, hoping to drive around the police car in his way, but Dalesia stopped beside his door and fired twice from the hip directly into the doorlock. On the other side, McWhitney showed his weapon to the guard but didn't fire it.

The armored car stopped. Dalesia tugged on the door he'd hit, and it eased open, and Dalesia went nuts, screaming, '*Out of there!*' Like a maniac, like someone barely under any kind of control, he screamed again before the men in the truck could react to the first order, '*You wanna die? You wanna die? I'll blow your fucking heads off.*' Then he made a high keening sound, like a banshee, and aimed the Commando at the driver's face.

'I'm coming! I'm coming! Here I come, take it easy, honest to God — '

As the driver and then the guard climbed

out, both on the driver's side, McWhitney ran back to deal with the third guard.

'Over there! Over there!'

Dalesia, jumping around as though he couldn't control his legs, pointed at the dirt road that angled off from here, and the two guards moved towards it. Parker came around the back of the police car, carrying the handcuffs, as Dalesia made the two lie face-down on the road and McWhitney brought up the third, who'd come out of his compartment without trouble.

The three were handcuffed, and then Parker ran back to the police car, Dalesia to the armored car, and McWhitney to the Celebrity. In that order they drove away from there, only Parker showing headlights, the other two staying close, guided by his lights.

It was fifteen minutes to the factory, where the rented truck waited for them. Parker and McWhitney wiped down the cars they'd been driving, while Dalesia backed the armored car around to the open back of the truck. Then they looked to see what they had.

The interior of the armored car was less than two-thirds full, and a quarter of that was canvas bags, which would be coins. They didn't want the coins. Dalesia, climbing up into the armored car as McWhitney shone a flashlight into it, lifted the lid off one of the boxes, and they all saw the neat stacks of green.

Dalesia laughed. 'My favorite color,' he said, and put the lid back down on the box, and they started the transfer.

Dalesia, staying in the armored car, moved each box to the rear door, Parker lifted it over the space to the truck, and in the truck McWhitney stacked them all.

The whole operation took less than ten minutes. Then Dalesia got behind the wheel of the truck and said, 'I'll see you there.' He drove out, and that left only the illumination from the interior light of the rental Dodge, with the driver's door open.

'We'll give him a couple minutes,' Parker said.

They leaned against the side of the pickup, and McWhitney said, 'I like that Carl-Gustaf. You point it at something, the thing stops.'

'Briggs earned his cut,' Parker said. 'We can go now.'

But as they turned away, they heard a distant flapping sound, high and repetitive. They looked at each other, and Parker said, 'Helicopter.'

'That was fast.'

'Everybody's on alert,' Parker said. 'Maybe we shouldn't be two cars traveling together.'

McWhitney nodded. 'You want me to go first?'

'You remember the way?'

'I'll find it.'

McWhitney climbed into the pickup and drove out of the building. As he left, the flapping sound got louder, though never directly overhead, and then it got softer again, and then it faded out. When it was gone, Parker got into the Dodge and drove out to the black night, switching on his headlights once he was on the road.

He hadn't gone far when the flapping sound came back, and this time he saw them: two long, narrow floodlight beams angled down from beneath two helicopters, one behind him near the scene of the robbery, the other up to his left, in case they'd continued northward.

The one from behind was coming this way. Parker drove steadily, and the finger of light illuminated trees and houses in his rearview mirror, closer and closer. He kept going, and the light approached him, then angled away to his right, hovering beside him a minute, so the people up there could study his car without blinding him. Then it swung on out to the front and moved ahead.

A few minutes later, as the two floodlights still walked like laser stilts across the night, Parker passed Dalesia in the truck, stopped and lightless beside a closed gas station. He was waiting for the helicopters to leave, knowing they'd be too interested in any truck-sized vehicle moving around in this area right now.

The light to the left disappeared first, and then the one straight ahead veered rightward and also disappeared. When Parker reached the church and drove around behind it, McWhitney paced back and forth just outside the lean-to, looking irritated. Parker opened his window and said, 'What did you do with your pickup?'

Pointing farther back behind the church, McWhitney said, 'There's some trees back there.'

Parker steered that way, saw the pickup nosed in among some scrubby trees, and put the Dodge in the same area, though he doubted those trees would hide much in the daytime. Then he walked back to McWhitney, who said, 'You see Nick?'

'Yeah, he was getting out of the way. He'll be along.'

'I don't like how fast they're being,' McWhitney said.

3

Dalesia drove the truck in around the side of the church ten minutes later. With hand gestures, Parker and McWhitney guided him to maneuver the truck in deeply under the lean-to until its right side was an inch from the rear wall of the church. Then Dalesia climbed down from the cab and said, 'We made a stir.'

'Don't need it,' McWhitney said.

'No, we don't,' Dalesia agreed. 'But we got it. Let's get the tarp over this thing.'

Earlier, they had stashed in here, hidden beneath crèche figures, a gray canvas tarp that would not reflect the light. Now, with Parker holding a flashlight to guide them, Dalesia and McWhitney draped it over the top and hood and left side of the truck. Then Parker switched off the light, and McWhitney said, 'Now we go in the church, right? Wait it out.'

Dalesia said, 'Where'd you put your cars?'

'Back in the trees,' McWhitney told him.

'There's too many choppers out,' Dalesia said. 'Why not put them across the road, beside the house there?'

'It's empty,' McWhitney objected. 'The

locals are gonna know they don't belong.'

Parker said, 'Nick's right. From the helicopter, our cars look as though we're trying to hide. Next to a house, they're normal. Tomorrow, we'll get them out of here.'

'Not in the morning, though,' Dalesia said. 'This heat isn't gonna go away for a while.'

McWhitney said, 'I tell you what. I'll put my pickup in front of the church, and Parker puts his car next to the house across the street. That way, during the day to-morrow, I'm a guy doing maintenance and he's the real estate broker.'

Dalesia laughed. 'I like your story lines,' he said. 'Parker?'

'Sure.'

They stepped out from under the lean-to, but then, from far off to their right, they heard the flap-flap again, and moved back inside. The helicopter never came close, but the noise of it ricocheted from the ground for about three minutes, while that thin vertical light moved over there like a pendulum made of a fluorescent tube.

At last the helicopter moved on, out of sight and out of sound, and then they moved the cars, Parker leaving the Dodge in front of the separate garage at the end of the driveway on the left side of the house.

He was about to turn back when he saw headlights approaching from the right, the same direction they'd come from. He dropped to the ground beside the Dodge and watched a car with a bubble light on top, unlit, hurry by; SHERIFF could be faintly read on the door.

After the sheriff's department car left, Parker stood and went back across the road, where Dalesia had the church front door open and called to him, 'Come in over here.'

It was very dark inside the church. There were too many large windows down both sides to permit them to use a light. Parker shut the door behind himself and spoke into the dark: 'That was a sheriff's car.'

'Well, they're out and about,' Dalesia said. 'You got that flashlight?'

'For what?'

'There's got to be a basement in here,' Dalesia told him. 'For Boy Scout meetings, ladies' auxiliary, AA.'

McWhitney said, 'Maybe the coffeemaker's still there.'

Parker held his fingers over the flashlight lens, switched it on, separated the first two fingers slightly, and by that faint light they moved around the church, which had wide straight lines of dark wood pews and a central aisle, a railing across the front, and beyond it

294

a bare plaster wall. Whatever altar and decorations had once been there were gone.

A door to the left of the entrance opened on stairs up to a pocket choir loft and down to a U-turn a half flight below. 'That's what we want,' Dalesia said.

It was. They went down, past the U-turn in the stairs, and below the church was a long, low-ceilinged rectangular room with cream walls and a pale, worn linoleum floor. Shelves and counters filled the wall along the back, amid spaces where stove, refrigerator, and dishwasher had been. The double sink was still there, but when they twisted the faucets, nothing happened.

The most interesting part was the windows, narrow horizontal ones down both sides of the room, high up near the ceiling, that cranked out and up. To each window had been added two narrow wooden strips, attached to the wall above and below the window, with a sliding cream-painted sheet of thin plywood between that could be moved either to block the window or to clear it. The system looked crude and homemade, but effective.

Looking at the windows, Dalesia said, 'They showed movies down here. Close them, we're gonna be fine.'

They slid all the plywood panels shut, and

McWhitney said, 'Shine your flash on a couple windows on that side, I'll go up and see does anything show through.'

He was gone, up into the darkness, for about three minutes, while Parker shone the light at two of the ply-wood panels, and when he came back down, he said, 'Dark as hell up there. Nothing showed.'

'Good,' Dalesia said.

'Also,' McWhitney said, 'another chopper went by.'

'Not good.'

'You know it. I just got back inside before the light went right over this place.'

Dalesia said, 'It did? We didn't see a thing.'

'So that's good, then,' McWhitney said, and looked around, saying, 'Do you suppose the power still comes in here?'

'The panel's back there, where the refrigerator used to be,' Dalesia said, and they went back to take a look. When they opened the circuit breaker box, the main switch at the bottom had been moved to Off, and all the circuit switches were also set at Off. A paper chart pasted to the inside of the metal door showed which breaker ran which circuit.

Dalesia studied the list. After a minute he said, 'Rec. That would be rec room, right? Suppose there's any law going by out there?'

McWhitney said, 'I'll go up. When I get

there, you throw the switch. If I holler, switch it off again.'

'Good.'

Parker said, 'Let's make sure something's on,' and he walked back to the stairs with McWhitney, where a set of four light switches was mounted on the wall. He flipped one of them up and said, 'We'll see what happens.'

'Give me a minute,' McWhitney said, and went away upstairs. Parker stayed by the light switches, and Dalesia, with Parker's flashlight, stayed by the circuit breaker box.

McWhitney called down, 'Try it now.'

Parker said to Dalesia, 'He says, now.'

Dalesia moved first the main switch and then the circuit breaker switch marked 'rec,' and fluorescents in the dropped ceiling, down at his end, began to sputter into life. Parker called up to McWhitney, 'It's on. Anything up there?'

'Nothing.' McWhitney came back down and said, 'I had to close the door at the top of the stairs, some light comes up there. But now we'll be fine.' Looking out at the rec room, he said, 'Snug. We're gonna be snug.'

Parker flipped on one more switch, so now they had pockets of light at both ends of the room. Dalesia came over to give Parker back his flashlight and to say, 'No coffeemaker, though. In fact, no water.'

'We got bottled water and candy and stuff stashed out back,' McWhitney said. 'And now we got light and a roof down here. Come on, we'll get the stuff and bring it down, and then we'll just wait it out till morning, see what we got then.'

They started for the stairs, Parker flicking on the flashlight, and Dalesia paused to say, 'You know what we got here? It's not just light and a roof. We're in a church, Nels. What we got, we got sanctuary.'

4

Parker woke first. The original idea had been, they would come here and divvy the boxes from the truck right away, Dalesia taking Jake's piece with him, Parker taking Briggs's. They might sleep a while in the vehicles, but then they would leave early in the morning. McWhitney would drive the rental truck, because his name was on the paperwork, while Dalesia would take McWhitney's pickup with his and McWhitney's shares in it. Parker, finished, would head home, while McWhitney dropped off the truck at a nearby office of the rental company and then drove Dalesia to the municipal parking lot in Rutherford where the Audi had been left.

Except it wasn't going to work like that. Law enforcement in recent years had come to expect an attack from somewhere outside the United States, that could hit anywhere at any time and strike any kind of target, and they'd geared up for it. Because of that, the few hours Parker and the other two had been counting on weren't there.

They couldn't leave this place, not yet, not with the money from the bank on them, but they couldn't stay here either. Having electricity all by itself wasn't enough. They needed food, they needed water, and they needed a better place to sleep than a wooden pew in the church, which was at least a little less hard and cold than the linoleum floor downstairs.

When Parker opened his eyes, lying on his back on the pew, pale early morning light gleamed in through the windows on the left side of the church, and darkness seemed to be drawn out through the windows on the right. His body stiff, he sat up and saw that Dalesia and McWhitney still slept on nearby pews. He got to his feet, stretched, bent, and then went to the front door. He opened it, made sure no traffic was going by, then went out, moved around to the rear of the church, relieved himself, and washed face and hands with bottled water. Far away, he heard the flap-flap, but then it faded.

Back inside the church, he went up to take a look at the choir loft, and saw that it had a round window at the back, above the front door. As he looked out through it, a state police car drove by. He watched it, then stepped back and looked at the space.

It was very cluttered. As wide as the church below, it was a narrow area with a railed opening at the front, above the main church.

At one time, it had been lined with rows of wooden folding chairs. These, along with a lot of cardboard boxes of the same sort as the ones they'd taken from the bank, were now stacked up almost everywhere. Parker opened one of the boxes, and it was full of hymnals, heavy books with thick shiny paper and speckled dark red covers.

Was there anything to do with these boxes? They weren't exactly like the ones from the bank, though very similar. It was a style of box with a separate cardboard top and fairly long sides that was sold to be used as storage. A dull white, they had handholds cut into the two narrow ends. When television showed U.S. marshals carrying evidence into federal courtrooms, they used these boxes.

How could Parker and the others make use of these things? Put a top layer of hymnals over the cash underneath? But at a roadblock, any cop was likely to lift at least one book.

Parker heard movement downstairs, looked over the front railing, and saw the other two starting to rouse. Dalesia looked up, saw him, and said, 'Anything interesting up there?'

'I don't think so.'

Parker went downstairs, and McWhitney said, 'After I go out and take a leak, I'll drive somewhere and find us something to eat.

Then we gotta figure out what we're gonna do around here.'

'How we're gonna get away from here,' Dalesia said.

McWhitney shook his head. 'With the profits? I don't think so. I'll be back.'

'I'll walk you out,' Dalesia said.

They left the building, and Parker went back downstairs, switching on the lights. There were closets and cabinets down here, and a storeroom and a room with the furnace and water heater. Parker searched everywhere and found nothing of use. Anything that could be removed without structural damage had been taken out of here.

He went back upstairs, and Dalesia was in the choir loft. He called down, 'You see these boxes?'

'Yeah.'

'Like ours.'

'Doesn't help.'

'Yeah, I know. Only it's like a coincidence.'

Except it wasn't; those were the boxes you got when you needed boxes and when, like a bank or a church, you didn't get your boxes from your neighborhood liquor store.

Dalesia came downstairs. Inside the chipper manner, he looked worried. 'It wasn't supposed to go like this,' he said.

'I know.'

302

'We were supposed to get out right away.'

'We couldn't.'

'But the longer we stick around, the worse it gets. What if it's a week before they call off the search?' With a gesture at the open, empty church, he said, 'We can't stay *here* that long.'

'I know it.'

'We don't have a base, Parker,' Dalesia said. 'We need a base.'

'We need to get *out* of here,' Parker said.

★ ★ ★

McWhitney brought coffee and pastries and news: 'I heard it on the radio in the pickup; they got Jake.'

The three were sitting on pews at the front of the church to eat their breakfasts. Dalesia said, 'What do you mean, they got Jake? He's in the hospital.'

'He went outa there last night,' McWhitney said. 'Don't ask me why. The cops found him this morning, wandering around in his hospital pj's. They said he was disoriented.'

'Sounds it,' Dalesia said.

'But then,' McWhitney said, 'they said he was cooperating.'

'Oh?' Dalesia frowned. 'Disoriented *and* cooperating?'

'His sister's with the cops,' McWhitney

said. 'She's the one they quoted on the radio. Her brother's cooperating.'

Parker said, '*She's* cooperating.'

'Sure,' Dalesia said. 'Trying to help her brother, soften the blow.'

'Well, what do they know, those two?' McWhitney asked. 'They don't know me at all. They could describe you guys.'

Dalesia said, 'Jake could make a little trouble for me. Not for Parker. But I'll have to move around some.'

Parker said, 'They'll sink the wife.'

'Christ, they will,' Dalesia said. 'And the doctor, you think?'

Parker shook his head. 'The doctor didn't do anything. He thought he was gonna do something, but then he didn't have to. If he just keeps his mouth shut now, he's fine.'

McWhitney finished his coffee and threw the plastic cup at the wall where the altar used to be. '*He's* fine,' he said. 'What about us? Parker, every move we make outside this building is full of risk. The cops are *everywhere*. It said on the radio, they're bringing in cops from out of state. It said, if they don't find us in three days, maybe they'll bring in the National Guard. The weapons we used, and the fact it's a bank, the feds are part of it.'

Dalesia said, 'We've got to get out of this

part of the country. We've just got to.'

'You haven't been out there,' McWhitney told him. 'I was just a few minutes each way, stayed on little nothing roads, I was stopped twice, show ID, search the car, thank you very much. One of the cops, I said I'm headed back to Long Island, he gave me a friendly advice, stay away from the MassPike, it's a horror scene down there, roadblocks every exit, traffic backed up to Boston.' He laughed, without much humor. 'There's a lot of drivers out there this morning, Nick,' he said, 'don't like us guys at all.'

'But there's still no choice,' Dalesia said. 'We've still got to move on away from here.'

Parker said, 'The problem is the cash. We can't carry it, and we can't stay here, so the only thing to do, we leave it. We can scoop out a handful each, but that's it.'

McWhitney looked deeply pained. 'Leave it? After what we went through to get it?'

Parker said, 'You put even one of those boxes of cash in your pickup, on the seat beside you, or I put it in the trunk of my car, the first roadblock we come to we're done.'

'I know that, Parker,' McWhitney said. 'I was just out there. But there's got to be some way we can move that cash around the cops or through them or something.'

'Nothing,' Parker said. 'There's nothing.'

McWhitney hated this. 'So whadda we do, then? We just *leave* it all here? I can't walk away from that truck out there, Parker, I rented that in my own name. So what are we supposed to do, just dump it all out on the ground?'

'No,' Parker said. 'We stash it.'

Dalesia said, 'That's a lotta boxes out there, Parker. Where we gonna find to stash that much stuff?'

'The choir loft,' Parker said.

5

There was a windowless door on the right side of the church, down near where the altar had once stood. Outside the door was a small gray concrete slab, and two concrete steps going down to ground level. Wrought-iron railings on both sides had been broken off and taken away, leaving twisted iron stubs.

The door was locked, and would open inward. McWhitney went around to the outside, stood on the slab, and kicked it open. Then they started moving the boxes out of the truck, at first only as far as the side wall of the lean-to.

When the first part was done, McWhitney drove his pickup around to that side and left it next to the wall, just forward of the doorway, its front end toward the road. That would both explain the open door and hide their movements as they carried the boxes around and into the church.

After the last box had been lugged in and stacked on the front pews, McWhitney kicked the door shut again, because otherwise it kept sagging open. And now they started the third and final part of the move, which was the longest and the hardest.

First they shifted some of the chairs and hymnal boxes that were upstairs, crowding them all as far as possible over to the left. Then they started bringing up the money boxes, stacking them in the right corner, four high, with hymnal boxes stacked on top. When everything was upstairs, they rearranged the rest of the boxes and chairs again, so that at the end it had the same cluttered look as before, but more crowded.

The whole move had taken more than two hours. Downstairs again, sitting in the pews, drinking the last of the bottled water as they caught their breath, they were all quiet for a few minutes, until McWhitney said, 'I figure a month.'

'At least,' Dalesia said.

'We can't leave that stuff up there forever,' McWhitney said. 'You never know, they could sell the building for an antique shop, clear out the choir loft and hello, what's this?'

Parker said, 'We'll give it a month, then see how things look around here.'

McWhitney finished his water. 'Time to go,' he said. 'Nick, follow me while I turn the truck in, then I'll drive you to your car.'

'I'll shut down here,' Parker said.

Dalesia said, 'Don't anybody try to get in touch with me, I'm gonna be on the move. I'll call you two one of these days.'

'I'll be in my bar,' McWhitney said, 'unless that Sandra decides to shoot me, so we can keep in touch through me.'

Dalesia said, 'What's she gonna shoot you for? You're gonna make her rich with all that Harbin money.'

McWhitney grinned. 'Maybe she'd like to co-own a bar.'

McWhitney and Dalesia left, McWhitney leading in the rental truck. After they were gone, Parker went through to remove things that might identify them later on, like coffee cups and water bottles. Everything went into the bag McWhitney had brought breakfast in.

He also went downstairs to be sure nothing had been left behind. He shut off the power, and used his flashlight to get back up to the main floor.

Finished with the church, Parker went to the front door, looked out, saw that the road was empty, and crossed over to the Dodge, which he'd left parked next to the empty house. He drove off, and the first town he came to, four miles away, he threw away the bag in a municipal trash barrel. Except for four thousand dollars in cash in his pockets, he was carrying nothing with him that he hadn't brought here.

It was seven miles farther on that he saw

his first roadblock, up ahead. It was positioned where a driver coming this way wouldn't be able to see it until he was close enough to be seen, with no turnoffs.

This being a small road with little traffic, the cops weren't dealing with anybody else at that moment, so all four of them, two each for the east and westbound lanes, waved him down. One looked at John B. Allen's identification while another checked the trunk.

Parker said, when he got his ID back, 'Where can I find a diner? I'm looking for lunch.'

'Sorry, pal,' the cop said. 'We're not from around here. Just keep on, you'll find something.'

Parker kept on.

6

Staying north of the MassPike, but still meeting roadblocks now and again, and with more than the usual traffic on these secondary roads, Parker traveled as due west as he could, figuring to leave Massachusetts and drive well into New York State before turning south. He wanted to get out of the search area as fast as possible, but he did need to eat.

The diner he found was still in Massachusetts. They had placed a television set on the back counter, because an Albany station was doing a special on the robbery and the search for the 'bandits,' as they called them. Parker gave his order, looked at the television screen, and the first thing he saw was Dr Madchen.

It was some sort of press conference, a podium in front of a blank yellow wall. Standing at the podium was the doctor, with a hangdog expression on his face, and a balled-up white handkerchief in his right hand that from time to time he pressed to his eyes. Standing beside him was a thirtyish woman, slender, with severe good looks and black hair in a bun. She wore a black broad-collared suit and high-neck white blouse, and it was soon obvious she was the doctor's lawyer.

A number of reporters were apparently out of sight behind the camera. When Parker first looked at the screen, the doctor was answering a question from one of them:

'I just feel so sorry for poor Jake right now. I know he tried to reform himself, I sincerely know he sincerely wanted to live a good life. If my own personal tragedy hadn't just now occurred — I mean, it's so hard for me to think after what's just happened — if I could, I'd do what I could to help Jake. He's a weak man, I admit that, but he isn't a bad man. He was led into this, just led into it.'

One of the unseen reporters, male, asked, 'Do you think there's any chance the authorities will think *you* were involved, Doctor?'

Looking more surprised than worried, the doctor said, 'Well, I certainly hope not. I mean, I can't think why they would. I'm a doctor, not a — Why would those people even *want* me with them, those robbers?'

The lawyer leaned in at that point to say, 'We are in discussion with the authorities, and there is no doubt that Mr Beckham said some very strange things while he was in his delirium, when the police first talked to him.

We take those statements, from a delirious and apparently guilt-racked mind, at face value, which is to say none, and we expect the police will make the same evaluation. It is of course a terrible accident of timing. This is a moment when Dr Madchen should be permitted the solitude of his private grief. Instead of which, he cannot grieve for his departed wife, as anyone else would be able to, but has to defend himself against the ravings of a temporarily disordered mind.'

Another reporter's voice asked, 'Doctor, did your wife have a history of heart disease?'

'Not at all.' Dr Madchen could be seen to be overcome for just a moment as he lowered his head, dabbed the handkerchief against his eyes, and clung hard to the podium with his other hand. Then he took a deep breath, nodded out at the reporters, and said, 'I was not my wife's primary physician, of course. I've been on the phone with her regular doctor, and he did tell me things I hadn't known. That he had counseled Ellen about her eating habits, for instance, and the lack of exercise in her life. I'd been aware of all that, but I had never — Ellen was so *healthy*, and then all at once — ' And he lowered his head again.

Parker's burger and fries arrived. As he ate and watched the press conference, he remembered what the good doctor had said, that time in his car when Parker and Dalesia had told him to stay away from Jake. 'If this thing you two are doing doesn't happen, I'm going to die. I can't live. You're my last hope.'

'Yes, the police phoned me at seven thirty this morning,' the doctor was saying. 'They wanted to tell me to stay at home, because they were coming to interview me. They told me about poor Jake, but not at that time about those . . . things he was saying. I said I'd wait at home for them, and I went to tell Ellen, and that's when I . . . I found her.'

Parker ate his lunch. As soon as Dr Madchen had been told, in that phone call, that Jake had been picked up, he'd known, no matter whether the robbery worked out or not, there would be nothing in it for him. As he'd said, in that case, somebody was going to die. He'd thought he would be that somebody, but when it came down to it, he'd found a substitute.

Parker ordered coffee, and when he looked back at the screen, a commercial was ending, to be replaced by a black-and-white drawing of a head shot, faced forward, the kind of thing done by police artists based on the memory of eyewitnesses. Like all such drawings, the guy looked too mean to be true, glaring out at the television audience. Over the picture, a woman's voice was saying, 'One police officer in our area does seem to have encountered at least one of the robbers shortly before the crime took place.'

The television picture cut now to two women seated at a table, with a bank of television screens on a wall behind them, showing an array of news and sports scenes. The woman on the left, about forty, was metallically pretty, with ironed-on blonde hair, a lemon-yellow sports jacket, and pale yellow blouse. The woman on the right was the cop who'd braced Parker.

The first one made the introductions: 'I have with me now Detective Second Grade Gwen Reversa of Massachusetts CID, who seems to have tied together some of the loose ends in this case. Welcome, Detective.'

'Thank you.' Detective Reversa smiled, happy to be there, but showed she wasn't going to be overly impressed by her moment of fame.

'Detective Reversa, your encounter with the alleged robber began with your investigation of what seemed to be a very different case, did it not?'

'Yes, Sue. I was assigned to investigate the shooting of Jake Beckham. In a case like that, where there doesn't seem to be any reason for what happened, you want to talk to as many of the victim's acquaintances as possible, and one of those was Elaine Langen.'

'The most astonishing character in the whole event,' the other woman said, with a big happy smile. 'You could have had no idea, when you first went to interview Elaine Langen, that she was in the middle of a scheme to rob her own husband's bank.'

'No,' Reversa said, with her own little smile, 'that one was not going to occur to me. Nor that she was the one, in fact, who'd shot Mr Beckham, who it turned out was a former lover of hers.'

'Elaine Langen's gun had gone missing.'

'Yes, Sue, that was the first hint that the situation might not be as clear-cut as it seemed. And a car outside the house when I arrived she said belonged to a landscape designer. When I later saw that same car — '

'Which turned out to be stolen.'

'Yes, from New Jersey, but I didn't know that then, I don't think it had been reported yet. But since, by that time, I had the feeling there was something wrong with Mrs Langen, although I didn't yet know what, when I saw that landscape designer's car at another time, I decided to take a look at him.'

The other woman chortled over this. 'Some landscape designer, eh?' Then, looking at the camera, she said, 'This is Detective Reversa's memory of that landscape designer,' and the mug shot drawing came on again.

They think that's me, Parker thought, and studied it, as the interviewer's voice, over the picture, said, 'This is almost certainly one of the robbers.'

An 800 number appeared, superimposed over the drawing. 'If you see this man, phone this number. Rutherford Combined Savings has posted a one-hundred-thousand-dollar reward for the capture and conviction of this man and any other member of the gang, and the recovery of the nearly two million, two hundred thousand dollars stolen in the robbery.'

Parker looked up and down the counter. Half a dozen other people were gazing at the television set. None of them looked to be ready to go off and make a phone call. It seemed to him, if you told one of those people, 'This picture is that guy. See the cheekbones? See the shape of the forehead?' they'd say, 'Oh, yeah!' But if it wasn't pointed out, they'd just go on eating lunch.

The screen showed the two women again. The interviewer said, 'Detective Reversa, what was the result of your meeting with this man?'

'I obtained an identification, in the form of a New York State driver's license, in the name of John B. Allen.' She spelled it.

The interviewer nodded, and produced another smile. 'Detective, would you like to meet up with John B. Allen again?'

Reversa laughed. 'If I had the appropriate backup.'

'Check,' Parker said.

He paid and started for the door, then stopped. Outside, off to the right, a police car was stopped behind the Dodge. Parker studied the newspapers in the rack beside the entrance, and the police car moved away to the right and stopped again, at the end of the lot, facing the road.

John B. Allen. One computer talks to another, and it doesn't take long. He'd been moving through the roadblocks just ahead of the news. John B. Allen is wanted for robbery over here. John B. Allen rented a car over there. Let's find the car, and wait for Allen to come back to it.

That was the only identification he had on him. He had cash, but nothing else. He couldn't drive the Dodge away from here. He couldn't walk away from the diner onto a rural road past those cops, because they'd want to have a word with him.

The diner's parking area was across the front and both sides. The Dodge and the cops were to the right. Parker stepped out the door and turned left, walking as though to his car. When he made it around the corner of the diner and out of sight of the cops waiting for him, he looked ahead and saw that behind the diner was a patch of weedy ground, and then scrub trees like the ones McWhitney had hoped to hide his pickup in among, and then a slope upward into more serious woods, some of them already rich with fall's yellows and reds.

Casual but steady, Parker walked out away from the parking lot and toward the trees. No one noticed or called to him.

7

It starts with technology, but it still ends with tracker dogs.

At first, Parker climbed up the slope through the thin trunks of the second-growth trees, wanting only to get high enough to see without being seen. He moved left and right across the slope until he found a spot where he could look down and get a clear view of the diner and its parking lot. The Dodge was still there. So was the police car. He leaned against one of the thicker trees to wait and watch.

So the bank said they'd been hit for two million. He knew from experience that that would be a lie. Because of the insurance, the company that got taken down always pumped the loss by between a quarter and a third. The money hidden back in the church would be closer to one million five.

That was less than they'd expected. What would Dr Madchen have gotten out of it, if things had worked the way they were supposed to work? A third of Jake's third, less the piece for Briggs. Two hundred thousand at most, probably less. He was better off giving the wife a little injection.

Down below, one of the cops got out of the police car and went into the diner. It had been twenty minutes since Parker had come up here.

What he wanted to do now was wait for them to decide he'd gone away, seen their car, and decided to leave his own. Once they were gone, he could come back down and decide what to do next.

The cop was inside the diner ten minutes, and came out with a paper bag. He got back into his car, but it didn't move. Which meant they weren't going away. They were waiting for reinforcements. They were going to start the search from right down there.

Yes. When the police bus and the enclosed police van drove into the parking area a good half hour later, he knew what it meant, and turned away, moving uphill. He didn't have to stick around long enough to see the hounds come out of that van.

Soon he heard them, though. There was an eager echo in their baying, as though they thought what they did was music.

Parker kept climbing. There was no way to know how high the hill was. He climbed to the north, and eventually the slope would start down the other side. He'd keep ahead of the dogs, and somewhere along the line he'd find a place to hole up. He could keep away from the pursuit until dark, and then he'd decide what to do next.

He kept climbing.